STAMPEDE!

"Hey, that's her!" Frank shouted. "That's the girl I saw panning for gold yesterday!"

The young woman jerked her head around, then dug her boot heels into the sides of her horse to get away. The Appaloosa charged forward, nearly colliding with several other horses. As the animals were jostled together, a few reared and pulled off to the sides.

Standing in the street, Frank stared after the young woman. Without warning he heard a loud neighing sound behind him.

"Watch out!" a woman screamed from the curb.

Wheeling around, Frank froze in horror. A huge white stallion, frightened by Frank's unexpected presence, had reared up on its hind legs. The horse's front legs pedaled wildly in the air above Frank. At any moment its hooves would come down on his head!

Books in THE HARDY BOYS CASEFILES™ Series

Available from ARCHWAY Paperbacks

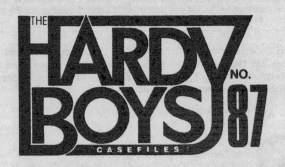

DEAD MAN IN DEADWOOD

FRANKLIN W. DIXON

AN ARCHWAY PAPERBACK
Published by POCKET BOOKS
New York   London   Toronto   Sydney   Tokyo   Singapore

AN ARCHWAY PAPERBACK *Original*

An Archway Paperback published by
POCKET BOOKS, a division of Simon & Schuster Inc.
1230 Avenue of the Americas, New York, NY 10020

Copyright © 1994 by Simon & Schuster Inc.
Produced by Mega-Books of New York, Inc.

ISBN: 0-671-79471-X

First Archway Paperback printing May 1994

10 9 8 7 6 5 4 3 2 1

THE HARDY BOYS, AN ARCHWAY PAPERBACK and colophon are registered trademarks of Simon & Schuster Inc.

THE HARDY BOYS CASEFILES is a trademark of Simon & Schuster Inc.

Cover art by Brian Kotzky

Printed in the U.S.A.

IL 6+

Chapter

1

"WELCOME to Black Hills National Forest, South Dakota," Joe Hardy announced, his head thrust out the window of the Hardys' black van. His blond hair was blown straight back as he read the large road sign flashing by.

"Thanks," his brother, Frank, said with a grin. "I'm sure with a little practice, you could get a job on South Dakota's tourist board."

"I'd take it," Joe said, pulling his head back inside the van. "Can you believe this scenery?"

Below and to Joe's right was a flat, semidesert plateau. The smooth, light pink and beige land stretched as far as Joe could see. Straight ahead, though, the lush, tree-lined Black Hills towered above the plateau, providing a sharp, green contrast. He imagined that the landscape was almost as it had been when the first white settlers came through over a hundred years earlier.

Joe turned to Frank. "I know we planned to drive straight through South Dakota, but we still have time until spring break's over. How about spending one night camping out here?"

"I promised Callie I'd be back in Bayport this weekend," Frank said. Callie Shaw, Frank's steady girlfriend, had been waiting for him to return from a video game convention in San Francisco. On the drive back east to Bayport, Frank and Joe had been camping in national parks and forests. But Frank knew they had to drive at least four more hours that day if they wanted to make Bayport by the weekend.

"I think Callie would tell you to spend an extra day exploring this country if you had the chance." Joe opened the guidebook in his lap. "They call the Black Hills the 'Foothills of the Rockies.' And look—the town of Deadwood is only a few miles from here."

"Deadwood?" As the van climbed up the steep, twisting road, the brush gradually became more dense. Frank could see large cliffs carved into the light-colored rock. "That sounds friendly."

"It's where the last big gold strike took place in the 1870s," Joe said, reading from the guidebook. "Overnight, a Wild West boomtown sprang up. Deadwood had gunfights, posses, shootouts on Main Street at high noon, the whole thing."

"Gunfights and shootouts," Frank repeated, nodding. "I can see where the *dead* in Deadwood came from."

"Practically everybody came through here," Joe continued. "Wild Bill Hickok, General George Armstrong Custer, Calamity Jane—Deadwood was like a Wild West Hall of Fame."

Frank eyed the road up the hill ahead of them. "This road is really getting steep," he muttered, concentrating on his driving. Then all at once he added, "Anything in that guidebook about buffalo?"

"Yep," Joe said, reading. " 'The Black Hills region has more buffalo herds than any section of North America.' "

"Good. Then I'm not hallucinating," Frank said as he headed into the next sharp turn.

Joe peered straight ahead. As the road bent around a curve, a green van sped toward them, then disappeared behind one of the hills. For a brief moment he saw a large buffalo following right behind the van, chasing it downhill at about fifty miles per hour.

"Wha—?" Joe began, staring wide-eyed at the space where the huge, shaggy animal had been. Frank burst out laughing.

"What's so funny?" Joe demanded. Frank pointed to the van, which had just reappeared on the winding road. As it moved downhill, Joe could see that the buffalo was an oversize stuffed replica, mounted on a flat trailer being towed by the van. He caught a quick glimpse of a large sign attached to the side of the stuffed buffalo: Deadwood Wild West Week. Fun for Everyone!

Joe groaned. "Very funny." Then he grinned. "But a Wild West Week sounds great, huh?"

Frank started to say something, then stopped. "Hey!" he said, scowling at the road ahead. The green van had drifted into their lane.

"He's going to hit us!" Joe cried.

Frank pulled as far as he could onto the right shoulder of the narrow highway, watching the three-thousand-foot drop off to his right. Just as the two vans seemed about to collide, the green van swerved back to its side, the trailer with the buffalo swaying violently from side to side.

As the van and trailer moved past, Frank glanced angrily over at it. The front windshield had been tinted, but through the open side window Frank spotted the driver, a young man with lank brown hair, a mustache, and a face that needed shaving. He was laughing. Two other young men were seated up front, and they were laughing, too.

"Real comedians," Frank said grimly. "Running people off a mountain road is hilarious." He glanced in the rearview mirror. The van and its trailer roared down the hilly road, out of sight. Frank hit the gas and continued the drive uphill.

Joe nodded. "I'd like to find those jokers and—" He stopped and cocked his head slyly. "Of course, if we stop near Deadwood for the night, we just *might* find them."

Frank shook his head in defeat. Joe was only a year younger than Frank, but sometimes he was as stubborn as a two-year-old. Looking ahead, Frank saw a fork in the road at the top of the next rise. One sign pointed east, in the direction of the interstate that would continue back toward the east. The other sign pointed north toward the campsites in the forest. With a loud sigh, Frank turned the van north.

"Yes!" Joe said triumphantly. "Now take the left here. There should be a campground about six miles up on the right, and Deadwood's maybe five miles north of that."

"Not that you had this all mapped out or anything," Frank said.

Joe shrugged and put the guidebook away. "Well, as Dad always says—being prepared is half the battle."

The drive north to the Black Hills National Forest campgrounds took the Hardys gradually up. The road began leveling off as they approached the camp entrance. They joined a short line of campers and minivans waiting to buy overnight passes.

Suddenly a loud siren blared from behind them. A voice boomed through an amplified speaker. "Stay to your right, please, coming through on the left!"

As Frank maneuvered the van to the right, the siren grew louder. Moments later a green-and-white National Forest patrol car raced past on the left. By habit, Frank noted the car's number—333. Its siren faded as it disappeared into the campsite ahead.

"Wonder who—or what—they're after?" Joe asked as the Hardys approached the entrance.

"Who knows?" Frank replied. "Maybe the ranger up there can tell us."

A young, red-haired woman in a Forest uniform was in the admission booth. She smiled hello as Frank handed her a bill. As she was making change, Frank said, "Excuse me, ma'am, but we were wondering why that patrol car was racing through here. Is there some kind of emergency?"

"Beats me," she replied, handing Frank his change. "But whatever it is, you can be sure it's under control. We probably have the best patrol force in the national park system."

"Well, that's reassuring," Joe said, leaning over Frank to smile at the girl.

She smiled back, her green eyes sparkling.

"Have a nice stay," she said to Joe as she handed Frank his change.

Frank nudged Joe to his seat as the van moved on.

"I'm starting to really like the scenery around here," Joe said, glancing over at the admission booth.

"Joe, you're hopeless," Frank said, rolling his eyes.

Frank guided the van slowly along the crowded road. Every campsite they came to was occupied. Most of the campers were tired-looking parents with young children. A few places were taken up by students on spring break, reading in the cool forest shade, or elderly couples setting up their tents like seasoned campers. Frank began to wonder if they would find an open spot.

"We're almost to the end of the line," he said. The traffic had thinned out as the campers ahead of them grabbed the few remaining spots. Frank was about to suggest they try one of the motels along the interstate when Joe said, "There's one."

The unoccupied site lay at the very end of the road. It was surrounded by a large grove of tall pines and was nearly hidden. Frank saw a little stream a short distance away, winding through the trees and dropping down a slope.

"Perfect," Joe said. "Let's park and set up."

Within minutes they had parked and unpacked their tent, sleeping bags, and cooking equipment.

"I'll start cooking the franks and beans," Joe offered. "Why don't—"

"I know, I know," Frank said wearily. "I'll get the water."

Joe grinned as Frank grabbed the plastic water jug. Their routine was second nature.

Frank cut through the trees and stepped through the low underbrush to the gurgling stream. As he squatted down to fill the jug with cold stream water, Frank breathed deeply. He could feel himself start to relax after the long hours of driving.

A flash of light suddenly caught his eye. He jerked his head around and saw a dark-haired young woman about fifty yards upstream. She was kneeling beside the stream, holding a black metal object in her hand.

"Hi there," Frank called, standing up. "You camping around here?"

The young woman turned, startled. When she spotted Frank she jumped to her feet. Frank could see that she was very pretty, with straight, chin-length black hair. She was wearing faded jeans and a sweatshirt that read Black Hills State College. Frank smiled and pointed at the object in her hand. "Catch any big ones?" he asked.

The young woman's dark eyes grew wide as if she were afraid, and she took a large step backward. Then she hurriedly snatched a small backpack from the ground, turned, and dashed into the woods. In her haste, she dropped the metal object. "Hey, wait!" Frank called out. She was gone.

Frank walked upstream to the spot where the young woman had been kneeling. Bending down, he picked up the metal dish the girl had dropped. It looked like a giant pie pan, about as big around as a Chinese wok.

"I've got the tent all set up, two sleeping bags unrolled, the stove and pot all ready, and you still haven't finished getting the water?" Joe's voice cut through the stillness.

Still holding the pan, Frank turned to his brother. He told Joe about the frightened young woman. Joe studied the pan in Frank's hand. "You know what this looks like?" he said.

Suddenly a loud voice boomed out from behind them.

"Okay, fellas, hold it right there!"

Joe whirled around to see two Forest Patrol officers standing a few yards away. They were each holding a .38 handgun—and the guns were leveled at Frank and Joe.

Chapter

2

FRANK AND JOE stared down the barrels of the identical .38s.

The larger of the two olive-uniformed officers stepped toward them. "Son, don't you know that panning for gold on National Forest land is a felony?" he said in a high-pitched voice. The voice seemed comical in a body that was over six feet tall and two hundred pounds. A tag on the officer's uniform read Sgt. Burns, National Forest Patrol.

"We weren't panning for gold, officer," Frank said in surprise.

"Oh, really?" the smaller officer, a Sergeant Drake, said, pointing his gun at the contraption in Frank's hand. "Then what do you call that?" Drake spoke in a slow, gravelly voice, coolly checking out Frank and Joe like a marine drill sergeant. Though smaller than his partner, Drake had an air of authority about him.

Frank glanced down at the metal object he was holding. "I guess it *is* a gold pan," he said. "But I just found it here. I picked it up as you were arriving."

Drake stared at Frank and began to chuckle. "I guess next you're going to tell us you don't know how to pan for gold," the man said. His lined and freckled face didn't seem to move as he spoke.

"As a matter of fact, we don't," Frank replied.

"As a matter of fact," Drake mimicked Frank, "we got a report of a young person sighted panning for gold on this very spot just twenty minutes ago. How do you explain that?"

"There was a girl about my age here," Frank said. "She was kneeling by the river with this pan. I thought she was catching fish. When she saw me, she got scared and ran off. She must have dropped this by accident."

Drake slowly lowered his gun into his holster and nodded to Burns, who reluctantly did the same. "Describe the girl," Drake said. Burns took out a note pad and pen.

"About five foot seven, with a slim, athletic build," Frank said. "She had short black hair, brown eyes, and she was wearing jeans and a Black Hills State College sweatshirt."

"What are your names?" Drake asked.

"Frank and Joe Hardy," Joe spoke up.

As Burns wrote their names down, Drake said to Joe, "You didn't see the girl?"

Joe shook his head. "I was setting up our camp," he said, jerking his thumb toward the campsite behind them.

"Okay, Frank and Joe Hardy," Drake said, "I'm buying your story this time. But if we ever catch you with a gold panner on National Forest land again, you'll be telling it to a judge. Any gold found here belongs to the federal government. Understood?"

"Yes, officer," Frank replied.

"Good," Drake said. "Now, if you don't mind, I'll take this." He snatched the pan from Frank's hand. "Let's go," he added to Sergeant Burns, and headed back toward the patrol car parked a short distance away through the trees.

"Have fun, guys, but be good," Burns said, putting away his note pad and winking at the Hardys. "You don't want to get on the wrong side of Sergeant Drake. Oh, and if you should happen to see that girl again, leave a message at the Forest Patrol Center. We'll get back to you."

Frank nodded, and the officers got in their car and drove off. It was car 333, the same one that had passed them earlier.

Joe turned to Frank. "Nice work. I leave you alone for five minutes and you almost get arrested."

Frank was looking around the wooded area. "Wherever she went, she went fast," he said musingly.

"Who, the girl?" Joe asked. "Maybe she's done this before and knows how to get away."

Frank shook his head thoughtfully. "It was more than that. When I said hi to her, she reacted as if she had seen a ghost."

"Just you, bro," Joe said, slapping Frank on the back. "Now how about some food?"

Frank nodded absently, looking upstream. Who was she? he wondered. And where did she go?

Frank let out a small moan. He turned in his sleeping bag, blinking in the bright sunlight coming in the open flap of the tent. He checked the other bag. It was empty.

Joe's head popped into the tent. "Thought I heard a noise from in here," Joe said. "Come on, let's get going."

"What time is it?" Frank asked, stretching and rubbing his stiff back and neck.

"Nine-thirty. You've slept almost ten hours. I think that fourth hot dog knocked you out," Joe said with a laugh. He poked Frank's bag with his foot. "The wonders of Deadwood, South Dakota, await us."

With a groan, Frank rose, washed, and dressed. Within half an hour he and Joe were back in the van, headed north for the short trip to Deadwood. This time, Joe drove while Frank studied the guidebook.

"Look at page twenty-three," Joe said. "I figure the first places to see are the Black Hills Mining Museum, the Homestake Gold Mine—it's the largest operating gold mine in the United States—then Mount Moriah Cemetery, where Wild Bill Hickok's buried. Also we can't miss the famous Saloon Number Ten, where Wild Bill got shot in the back—"

"Hold it!" Frank said. "We're spending a few hours here, not the rest of the month."

"Hey, what's that?" Joe asked, nodding his head to the right.

Frank glanced out the passenger window. The drive north had been a continuous descent. Now they were only a few hundred feet above a flat, desertlike plateau. Small boxy buildings dotted the area, and a few people could be seen around the gathering of randomly spaced structures.

"That must be the Indian reservation," Frank said. Joe pulled off the road and stopped. Traffic moved past them as Frank consulted the guidebook. "According to the book, it's the Black Cloud Indian Reservation. It was established in 1868, and its members belong to the Lakota Sioux Nation. Right now it's only thirty-six square miles in size, but more land is supposed to be returned to the Black Cloud tribe at a later date, according to a treaty."

"The Sioux were terrific fighters," Joe said. "They're the ones who defeated Custer at Little Bighorn."

"And I believe that was their last victory," Frank added. "After that, even the warriors were forced onto reservations like this one."

"Doesn't seem fair," Joe said.

They stared down at the flat, barren area. The wide spaces and open sky made the scattered buildings and scrub brush seem small and lost.

Finally Joe started the engine, and they continued to Deadwood. Within five minutes they were entering the bustling tourist town.

"Wow, look at this place!" Joe said. "It's bigger than I expected." In contrast to the reservation, Deadwood was packed with people and cars and bustled with activity. Joe headed down Main Street, which was lined with wooden storefronts right out of the 1870s. Hotels, a newspaper office, a telegraph office, a sheriff's office, saloons, a gold claim stake office, and a bank with bars on the windows rose up on either side of the street.

"It's like stepping right into a western movie," Joe said.

Frank nodded but noticed, too, that interspersed among the Old West fronts were a few more modern ones. Most had been disguised to match the older buildings but were there to serve Deadwood's current residents. These included restaurants, gas stations, a laundromat, and two banks. Banners hung across several of the storefronts, proclaiming Deadwood Wild West Week. Fun for Everyone!

Tourists were wandering up and down Main Street, clutching shopping bags and cameras. A number of people, most likely locals, Frank thought, were dressed in Old West attire—boots, chaps, string ties, and broad-brimmed Stetson hats.

There were also a good number of Native Americans on the street, Frank noted, probably from the Black Cloud reservation. Several were dressed in traditional Sioux attire, with breech cloths and buffalo vests. Their hair was plaited in two braids. Maybe, Frank thought, this was why the reservation had seemed so deserted. Many of the Black Cloud Sioux must be in Deadwood for Wild West Week.

"There's the Gold Rush Museum," Joe was saying. "And there's the Ghosts of Deadwood Gulch Wax Museum. Oh, and there's the Buffalo Museum! Where do we start, Frank?" Joe asked.

Frank scanned the map of Deadwood in the guidebook. "I think we should head for the north end of town," Frank said. "Stay on Main

16

Street until we come to Saloon Number Ten. Then we'll park and walk around from there."

"Good plan," Joe said. A few moments later the saloon appeared on their right. Joe pulled past it and into a public parking area behind the row of buildings. The Hardys stepped out into the hot, dry sun and started back toward the saloon.

"According to the guidebook, Bill Hickok was playing poker in this saloon, with his back to the front door, when Jack McCall sneaked in and shot him in the back," Frank said.

"Right," Joe said. "He was holding two aces and two eights when he was shot. Ever since, that hand's been known as a 'dead man's hand.'"

"Remind me not to play poker in Deadwood," Frank said with a laugh.

Saloon #10 was a few doors up the block. "At least there are no crowds here," Joe said. Indeed, that side of Main Street was empty, but across the street, people were lined up six and seven deep. They all seemed to be staring at the Hardys.

Suddenly the blast of a gunshot rang through the air. The noise made Frank jump. The swinging doors to Saloon #10 burst open, and a man in a tattered vest and Stetson hat came racing out of the saloon. He was waving a smoking gun.

"They'll never take me alive!" he shouted.

17

He turned and ran past the Hardys into the middle of Main Street.

"That guy just shot someone!" Joe cried as five or six other men burst out of the saloon with guns drawn. All of them were dressed in western gear.

"Don't let him get away!" one of the men yelled. The group raised their guns, taking aim at the lone gunman, who was now behind Frank and Joe.

Frank realized all at once that he and Joe were right in the line of fire. "Hey, wait!" he shouted. He tackled Joe, and the two hit the dusty ground just as gunfire started blazing over their heads.

Chapter
3

THE HARDYS COVERED their heads as shots rang out and the smell of gunpowder filled the air. Suddenly a voice shouted, "Okay, I surrender!"

"Grab the no-good varmint!" one of the gunmen yelled. The shooting stopped. Frank and Joe cautiously uncovered their heads and struggled to their feet.

The men who had burst from the saloon had disarmed the lone gunman. As they hauled him away, the people lining the street cheered and laughed.

"What's going on?" Joe asked as he brushed dirt from his hands and arms. He looked over at Frank, who was wearing an embarrassed grin. "I think we goofed," Frank said.

As the tourists began to fill the street and sidewalks again, Frank pulled the guidebook out and turned to the description of Saloon #10. "Yes, here it is," he said. "Every day they re-create the shooting of Wild Bill Hickok. Jack McCall attempts a getaway only to be caught by a local mob. McCall is then taken to the old courthouse, where his trial is re-staged. All the characters are portrayed by local citizens of the Deadwood area. It's a very popular event with tourists."

"Not too popular with me," Joe grumbled, redfaced, rubbing his arm where he'd hit the street. "Someone could have at least told us," he added as they walked to the curb.

"Hey, you tenderfoots are lucky that wasn't the real thing," a voice behind them said. Frank and Joe turned to see a young man observing them. The stranger, standing with his thumbs hooked in the pockets of his low-slung, dirty jeans, laughed mockingly. His thin brown hair, straggly mustache, and face looked familiar to Frank. He realized all at once that the man was the same one who had been driving the buffalo trailer the day before. Two other young men stood behind him, and Frank suspected they were the same two who had been riding in the green van.

"Actually, that's our second close call in two days," Frank said. "Yesterday, driving into the

Black Hills, we almost got run off the road by some jerk driving a van with a buffalo trailer."

Instantly the smile disappeared from the young man's face. He and his buddies stared at Frank and Joe. "Gee, you sure are having all sorts of bad luck, aren't you?" the man said, then spit in the dusty road.

"Was it bad luck or bad driving?" Frank retorted. "If I'm not mistaken, you were there."

"Are you accusing Slim Davenport of being a reckless driver, friend?" the man asked, edging closer to Frank.

Joe stepped right up in front of him. "If you're Slim Davenport, then that's exactly what he's doing," Joe said, his eyes flashing.

"Then he's a liar," Slim said. "Because if I'd wanted to run someone off a road, believe me, he wouldn't be standing here now, talking about it. That's how good a driver I am."

Frank stepped up and held Joe back by the arm. "I'm Frank Hardy," he said, "and this is my brother, Joe. I don't believe we caught your friends' names."

"Doug Pitman," the shorter of the remaining two said. He spit out a small squirt of tobacco juice.

"Rob Mitchell," the other one said.

"Well, Slim, Doug, and Rob, you know what Joe and I are going to let you do?" Frank asked. "We're going to let you apologize for almost running us off the road yesterday."

Slim stared at Frank. Then he broke into harsh laughter. His two friends followed suit. "No, I tell *you* what," Slim said, still laughing. "We're gonna let *you* apologize to us for making a false accusation."

"Can't do that, Slim," Frank said, feeling Joe tense up. "That'd be lying."

Suddenly a high-pitched voice called out, "Hey there, Slim. You behaving yourself?"

Frank turned to see Sergeants Burns and Drake walking down the sidewalk. Both men were in casual dress, instead of their uniforms.

"Hi, officers," Slim said warmly, smiling at the two men. "We're just getting acquainted with two new tourists to our fine town."

Drake stared at the group. "Yes," he said suspiciously. "We got acquainted with the Hardys yesterday at the campground. Did anything else unusual happen after we left you?" he asked, turning his gaze on Frank and Joe.

Frank shook his head. "I didn't see the girl again, or I'd have called you."

Burns nodded and smiled at the group. "It's nice to see young folks from around here being helpful to tourists." Burns focused on the Hardys. "Bet Slim told you not to miss the rodeo starting in a little while." Slim's and Frank's eyes met.

"I was just getting around to telling them about the rodeo, Sergeant," Slim said. "We want the Hardys to come to our rodeo. We promise to put on a special show just for them." Slim glanced at his watch, then at Doug and Rob. "We'd better get a move on, guys, or we'll be late."

"Okay, Slim," Burns said. "And good luck shooting today." Slim smiled and nodded, then he and his friends moved off.

"Shooting?" Frank asked.

"Slim's one of the best dead-eye shots in the Dakotas," Burns told Frank. "Look for him to win a first prize at the rodeo."

"I'd be careful about doing too much socializing with Slim and his crew," Drake added. "Slim's had his share of scrapes in this town. In fact, one more driving violation and he'll have his license suspended for two years."

Frank and Joe exchanged a quick glance. "Where does the rodeo take place?" Frank asked.

"Right here in town, just a little ways east on Main Street. You can't miss it," Burns replied. "Maybe we'll see you there."

As Burns and Drake moved off toward a restaurant down the street, Joe said to his brother, "Slim must have quite a reputation. Even the Forest Patrol knows him. I know if I'd spent one more minute with Mr. Personality I'd have . . ." His voice trailed off.

"He's not exactly the welcoming committee I was hoping for, either," Frank said wryly.

"What do you say we find a friendlier part of town?"

"How about a place that serves breakfast?" Joe suggested.

Frank spotted a little diner tucked between an Old West supply store and a western hotel. An old sign across the front read Murph's Place. Frank lifted his eyebrows at Joe in question. Joe nodded. "Murph's it is."

The few tables in the small, well-scrubbed restaurant were taken, so Frank and Joe sat at the counter and began looking over the plastic-coated menus.

A little old man in a western shirt and an apron approached from behind the counter. "It's all good, boys. But my specialty is franks 'n' beans," he said. Frank made a slight grimace as Joe laughed.

"I think we'll go for the ham and eggs with side orders of fries," he told the man, whose skin had the texture of well-worn leather. "By the way, are you Murph?"

"I'd better be," the man said, shuffling back toward the kitchen. "I'm wearing his clothes and living in his house." Frank and Joe laughed as Murph disappeared into the back of the restaurant.

It wasn't long before the Hardys were diving into the best ham, eggs, and fries they'd tasted since leaving Bayport. Murph leaned against the counter and gazed at the tourists who passed by the front windows of the restaurant.

"The town's sure packed with tourists," Frank commented. "We barely found a camping spot."

"That's only because of the Wild West shindig John Pressel dreamed up," the old man said. "We do okay during the winter ski season and summers from June to Labor Day, but spring and fall can get pretty slow around here."

"Who's John Pressel?" Frank asked. "The mayor?"

"Nah—he's the largest land owner in the Black Hills. Plus he sits on the board of the town bank," Murph told him. "He even came up with a big idea about building a Wild West theme park near here to keep the crowds coming off-season. He's got the whole town believing it'll make Deadwood a boom area year-round."

"Sounds like it could," Frank said. "You don't agree, Murph?"

"It could," Murph said, pulling on his chin. "I only hope it helps the *whole* town, not just a few."

"Where do they plan on building this theme park?" Joe asked. He'd just cleaned his plate, and Murph tossed a few more fries on it.

"Piedmont Flat," Murph said. "Outside the forest, near the Black Cloud reservation."

"How does the Black Cloud tribe feel about that?" Frank asked.

Murph paused. "Can't speak for the tribe," he said. "But I can tell you one man who's not going to cave in to John Pressel. That's Dan White River, the chairman of Black Cloud's tribal council. Pressel wants to build most of the park on a big piece of his land next door to the reservation. But he's got a problem. That section of land is due to be returned to the tribe in about ten months, according to a treaty that goes back a hundred years."

"We read about it," Frank said, nodding.

"Well, what you didn't read," Murph said, "is that Dan White River has no intention of letting Pressel keep that land. Pressel's been trying for over a year to get the tribe to agree to sell it back to him once it's theirs, but Dan's in charge at the reservation and he won't budge. Dan's got his own plans for the land. And I say good for him!"

Just then loud band music and cheering erupted out on Main Street. "What's that?" Joe asked, turning to the front window.

"That'd be the rodeo parade, heading over to the rodeo grounds," Murph said. "It's quite a show. They dress up like folks did over a hundred years ago to give it that Old West flavor."

Joe moved over to the window while Frank finished off his meal. "Hey, Frank, our friend

Slim Davenport just walked by," Joe reported, "waving his six-shooter at the crowd."

Murph seemed surprised. "You fellas know Slim?"

"As well as we care to," Frank said with a slight frown.

"Be careful of that one," Murph said. "Sometimes he don't know it's not 1870 anymore."

"Frank, come here," Joe called over his shoulder. "You don't want to miss this." Joe was watching a group of Sioux tribe members on horseback, in particular a young woman riding an Appaloosa toward the rear. She wore breeches and a leather vest and had two stripes painted below her eyes. She was very pretty, Joe realized, even if her short black hair wasn't as traditional as her clothes.

Murph had moved to the window to watch. "Oh, that's Cathy White River, Dan's daughter. Smart as she is pretty, too. Studies geology and mineralogy at Black Hills State."

Mention of Black Hills State caught Frank's attention. He joined Joe at the front window. The girl on horseback was just approaching the front of the diner, while onlookers lining the sidewalk waved and cheered.

"Hey, that's her!" Frank shouted. "That's the girl I saw panning for gold yesterday by the stream!" Before Joe or Murph could react, Frank dashed out of the diner.

27

Pushing through the crowd, he reached the curb just as the girl passed by. "Hey, Black Hills State!" Frank shouted.

The young woman jerked her head around to see who had called out. She stared right into Frank's eyes. Frank smiled and made a panning motion with his hands. "Remember me?" he asked.

The young woman's mouth dropped open and she turned away quickly, then dug her boot heels into the sides of her horse to get away. The steed charged forward, nearly colliding with several other horses.

"Hey, wait, I just want to talk to you!" Frank called out. He jumped off the curb and ran after her.

The young woman's Appaloosa had upset the other horses in the parade. As the animals were jostled together, a few reared and pulled off to the sides.

Standing in the street, Frank stared after the young woman. Without warning he heard a loud neighing sound behind him. "Watch out!" a woman screamed from the curb.

Wheeling around, Frank froze in horror. A huge white stallion, frightened by Frank's unexpected presence, had reared up on its hind legs. The horse's front legs pedaled wildly in the air above Frank. At any moment its hooves would come down on his head!

Chapter

4

FRANK REMAINED ROOTED to his spot, unable to take his eyes off the rearing horse.

From out of nowhere, he felt two hands grab his shirt collar and yank him backward. As he fell into the crowd, the horse's front legs came crashing down to the street, hitting the exact spot where Frank had just been standing.

He let out a sigh of relief and turned to find Joe behind him, still holding a fistful of collar.

"Walking into a parade with horses—good thinking," Joe said sarcastically, leading Frank back to the diner.

Frank straightened out his shirt. "I didn't see them," he muttered.

"Yeah, who'd expect horses in a rodeo parade?" Joe asked, rolling his eyes.

The brothers paid for their ham and eggs, bid a farewell to Murph, and returned to their van to drive to the rodeo.

"Are you sure that was the same girl you saw at the campground?" Joe asked as Frank climbed behind the wheel to start the engine.

"I'm positive," Frank replied. "You don't forget a face like that."

"Callie wouldn't be pleased to hear you say that," Joe said with a smile.

"I'm just curious," Frank said, maneuvering the van out of the parking lot, "why she was so scared of me before—and this time, too? And why was the Forest Patrol so interested in knowing who was panning for gold?"

"Because it's illegal?" Joe put in.

Frank shook his head. "You saw that expression on her face. There has to be something else going on."

The rodeo grounds were just past Deadwood's downtown area, and twenty minutes later the Hardys had bought their tickets and passed through the front gate. The grounds were like a small, round football stadium, with bleachers set up around a fenced-in ring. The ring was filled with dirt and smelled of horse manure. Frank and Joe found seats near a railing at the far end of the grounds. At the other end, pens held horses and bulls waiting to perform.

"Ten dollars to get in, three dollars for a program, two dollars for a soda," Joe complained. "Looks like whoever's running this show is making out okay."

"Probably that Pressel guy Murph was talking about," Frank replied. "If Wild West Week was his idea, he probably has a piece of this, too." Frank glanced in the program. Indeed, there was a photo and story about John Pressel on the first page. Flipping through, Frank found Cathy White River listed in the women's calf-roping competition, which was scheduled for later in the program.

Frank looked around the stadium area. The stands were filled with tourists, many with stiff new cowboy hats perched awkwardly on their heads. There were also some local people, including some Native Americans and some veteran cowboys.

The buzz of the spectators died down quickly as two men approached a microphone stand set up in the center of the arena. One was a burly, middle-aged man in a suit and tie. He had gray hair and a flushed complexion. The other man was dressed in slacks, shirt, and leather vest, and his black hair was worn in two long, thick braids that hung down past his shoulders. He was shorter than the burly man, and his face was a dark, leathery brown. He appeared to be at least fifty years old.

A voice over a loudspeaker boomed out,

"Ladies and gentlemen, your cohosts for today's events, Mr. John Pressel and Mr. Dan White River!" The crowd applauded. Pressel smiled broadly and waved while White River nodded politely. Pressel stepped up to the microphone.

"Thank you, folks. Thank you all for coming. Your support today means a lot," he said. "Every nickel earned here this afternoon will be invested in the development of Deadwood Days. We've already started our groundbreaking out on the plateau, and when it's completed next year, we'll have the greatest theme park in America right here in the Black Hills!" The crowd applauded again.

"Deadwood Days means jobs and financial security for you, your children, and their children for years to come," Pressel continued, punctuating the words with a pointed finger. "Everyone in America's going to want to visit our park. And we're gonna let 'em come!" While the crowd continued to cheer, Frank noticed that Dan White River, standing off to Pressel's side, did not look impressed.

Pressel paused and then began speaking in a softer tone. "Not everyone has agreed that we need to build another tourist attraction like Deadwood Days. I respect that." White River stared directly at Pressel. "But I would say to you all that while the Black Hills have a great and proud past, it is the future we must look to. And that's what construction of Deadwood Days will guarantee. Our future!"

By now Pressel's voice was raised to a booming pitch again, and many in the stands were standing and applauding. Frank noted that most of the Lakota tribe remained seated, silently watching. "It is my hope that Deadwood Days will bring all the people of this region together. To help us build a common future and put past differences behind us.

"Now," Pressel said, gesturing across the ring, "to today's events. We're going to see some of the best rodeo talent east *or* west of the Rockies! And as an extra incentive to today's contestants, I'll be awarding one hundred shares of stock in Deadwood Days to the contestant judged best all-around. Now, for some final remarks, my good friend Mr. Dan White River."

To polite applause, the tribal chairman approached the microphone. His manner was more reserved than Pressel's. His words were carefully and thoughtfully chosen.

"Thank you, my friends," he said. "We of the Black Cloud Reservation are always eager to help the cause of goodwill in the Black Hills region. As Mr. Pressel mentioned, not all of us agree on what should be done with the land. We must remember that the land is a gift to us, which we must pass on to generations to come. How we use the land says much about who we are.

"But for now let's enjoy today's festivities. And allow me to remind you that the closing ceremony for this special week will be a reenactment of the Battle of Little Bighorn. It will be staged out on the Piedmont Flat area. I urge as many of you as possible to attend this historic re-creation. And now good luck to all."

White River stepped away from the microphone as the crowd applauded. Attendants came out to remove the mike and to clear the temporary stand.

"Here come the bronco riders!" Joe called out.

Frank stared down at the far end of the arena. A chute opened and a young wrangler, dressed in old-fashioned chaps and spurs, shot out on a roaring bronc as the crowd cheered. He was the first of several bronc riders, all of whom tried to stay on the wildly bucking horse for the required eight seconds. Only one succeeded. The crowd gasped as one contestant after another was thrown to the ground.

"Now, this should be good," Joe said, nudging Frank. The last contestant was Doug Pitman, one of Slim Davenport's pals. Doug and his horse seemed to be thrown from the chute, and Doug was barely able to hold on to the strap. In less than three seconds he was tossed to the ground. He almost caught the bronc's right leg square in the jaw as he scrambled for the fence and safety.

"I guess riding in a van is easier than riding a bucking bronc," Frank said with a grin.

Following a short break, the next event was the sharp-shooting competition. Three bull's-eye targets were lined up against a fence, ten yards apart. At a signal from the starter, a rider came out of a pen on his horse. Without stopping, the rider passed by each target, shooting his Colt .45 revolver at each one. Whoever scored the highest number of combined points on the three targets won the competition.

The first few competitors had difficulty hitting any part of the bull's-eye target, and the scores were low. "This is almost impossible," Frank said. "Hitting a moving target is tough enough. Hitting a target while *you're* moving is almost impossible."

It was time for the next competitor. "Ladies and gentlemen," the loudspeaker voice boomed. "From Deadwood, South Dakota, here's Slim Davenport!"

The chute opened and Slim, atop a jet black colt, came dashing from the pen. Without breaking stride he whipped out his .45 and took aim at all three targets. He scored a bull's-eye on each. The crowd went crazy. "How's that for shooting, folks!" the announcer boomed. With a cocky smile, Slim spun his .45 and tipped his cowboy hat to the crowd.

Frank and Joe were impressed. "Slim Davenport must spend a lot of time practicing," Frank mused.

To no one's surprise, Slim won the target-shooting event. Several other events followed, including stunt horseback riding, an obstacle race on horseback, which Slim also won, and a show by the curious clowns.

"We're up to calf roping—Cathy White River's event," Frank said. "Let's see if she strikes gold here." He leaned forward in his seat to watch the first two competitors. They roped their calves and had them on the ground in about ten seconds. Then it was Cathy's turn.

"Our next competitor likes to begin a little differently, folks," the announcer said. "Let's welcome Cathy White River of the Black Cloud Reservation."

Cathy walked out into the arena, dressed in jeans, boots, and a western shirt. A chute opened, and a brown and white horse appeared about fifty yards from Cathy. The young woman made a thumbs-up motion with her right hand. The horse froze in place, staring at Cathy. Then Cathy rolled her hands one over the other. Instantly, the horse tore off toward the young woman. As it reached her,

Cathy jumped onto the horse and the crowd roared its approval.

Cathy then shouted out, "Now!" The calf chute opened at the far end of the arena. Although she was starting farther away than the other contestants, Cathy raced toward the calf at lightning speed, spun her rope about the calf's neck, and had it on the ground and tied in under seven seconds. Cathy then untied the calf, and it got up and scampered away, unhurt. As the crowd cheered wildly, Cathy gave a modest wave of her hand and ran off.

"Wow!" Frank said as Joe whistled his approval. There were three more women competitors, but none came close to Cathy's time.

At the end of the competition, the arena was cleared and John Pressel and Dan White River again took center stage with a microphone. "Weren't they terrific?" Pressel said loudly as the crowd applauded.

"But there can be only one winner of the all-around award," Pressel said. "And that winner is—Slim Davenport!"

Loud cheers and shouts of "Slim! Slim!" greeted the lanky cowboy as he swaggered toward the microphone area. He doffed his hat to the crowd smugly. Pressel shook Slim's hand and handed him the stock certificate. Slim waved it to the crowd in triumph.

"Congratulations, Slim," Pressel said. "You're

holding a piece of Deadwood's future in your hand!"

Dan White River stood silently next to Pressel and Slim. Though his face still wore a calm, reserved expression, Frank noticed that his chest was heaving up and down as if it were about to explode.

The Black Cloud leader turned to Slim, who was still waving the certificate overhead like a trophy.

Suddenly Dan White River reached up, grabbed the stock certificate from Slim's hands, and ripped the paper in two. Then he tore the two halves in half and tossed the pieces to the ground.

"There will be no boomtown at the expense of the Sioux Nation!" White River said firmly into the microphone. "Not now, not ever!"

Chapter

5

THERE WAS A LOUD GASP, and then a stunned silence fell over the arena.

"You crazy old fool!" Slim shouted. "You just tore up a small fortune!" He charged Dan White River, knocking him to the ground.

"Hey!" Joe cried, leaping to his feet in the stands. "What does he think he's doing?"

The Sioux leader grabbed Slim by the trouser leg and yanked him to the ground also. The two men began trading punches to the ribs and face. Shouts and shocked murmurs ran through the crowd.

Then men began jumping over railings to run to the center of the arena where Slim and Dan were slugging it out on the dusty ground. Dan White River had not been able to get out from under the younger, quicker Slim. John Pressel stood off to the side, calmly watching.

"Come on!" Joe said. "Let's see if we can help."

As the announcer pleaded with people to stay in their seats, Frank and Joe jumped over the railing. Cathy White River had just entered the arena, but a spectator in a cowboy hat and jeans was trying to keep her away from the fight. "That's my father getting beaten up!" she shouted.

"You just wait over there, miss," the spectator said, grabbing Cathy by the arm.

"Let go of me!" Cathy cried.

"No, don't cause any more trouble here," the man warned.

"You heard her—let her go," Frank said as he and Joe ran up.

The man glared at Frank and Joe. "Who are you?"

Joe ignored him and brought his hand down in expert karate-chop style on the man's arm. The man let out a yell and released Cathy.

Then Cathy, Frank, and Joe raced toward the center. The men who had arrived before them were making only a halfhearted attempt to break up the fight. "Someone do something!" Cathy cried. "My father's getting hurt!"

Joe dove into the circle and landed on top of Slim. He pushed the young man to the side, allowing Dan White River to get up. Joe then grabbed a surprised Slim by the shirt collar and yanked him to his feet. Slim, breathing hard, grabbed Joe's shoulder. His two buddies, Doug and Rob, stepped forward as Frank moved up next to Joe.

"How about picking on someone your own age, Slim?" Joe said between clenched teeth. "Or don't you like the odds?"

With a sneer, Slim jerked himself out of Joe's grip. Then he bent down and picked up some of the torn pieces of the stock certificate. He turned to Dan White River, who was being tended to by Cathy.

Slim threw the torn pieces at White River. "You'll pay for this, old man. If I can't replace this, you're going to make good every penny coming to me." Slim nodded to his two buddies, and the three of them walked off.

Pressel quickly went to the mike. "Just a little flare-up, folks," he said, with a chuckle in his voice. "Nothing to get excited about. Now, if you want some real excitement, don't forget about the big postrodeo barbecue and picnic. Starts at five-thirty on the picnic grounds off Lincoln Avenue. See you all there!" Pressel let out a loud "yippee," then walked away from the mike. The men who had run out to the fight now started to filter back to the stands, which were quickly emptying.

Pressel strode over to Dan White River.

41

Cathy was gently dabbing a cut over her father's left eye with a handkerchief. Frank and Joe watched Pressel approach.

"Dan, that wasn't exactly a gesture of cooperation on your part, tearing up that stock certificate like that," Pressel said easily.

"That's right. It was a gesture of my noncooperation," White River said. "You know how I feel about the theme park and about your trying to buy the land back that we will finally reclaim."

"Yes, I know how you feel, Dan. But how does the rest of your tribe feel?"

"I am chairman of the Black Cloud tribal council," White River said firmly. "I speak for the tribe."

"You still have time to think this over, Dan," Pressel said. "It's a major decision—"

"And one I have already made," White River interrupted. "There is nothing more to discuss."

"We're going now, Dad," Cathy said, still holding the handkerchief to her father's wound. She turned to Pressel. "You've got your answer, Mr. Pressel." Then, turning her back on him, she led her father off toward an arena exit.

"Aren't you going to talk to her?" Joe asked his brother as Pressel also turned away.

"I tried," Frank replied. "But there were too many people around. I couldn't even get her attention." As Frank spoke, he noticed that Pressel had begun a whispered conversation with a young man dressed in the traditional Sioux clothing worn by many of the participants. Pressel was doing most of the talking. The young man nodded, his handsome face grave, then whispered something into Pressel's ear. Pressel nodded, smiled, patted the young man on the back, and walked off.

"Wonder what that was all about," Frank said. The young man had now joined several other members of the tribe, one dressed in traditional garb and the others in jeans and western shirts. Like him, they were all in their twenties. After the young man spoke to them, they all headed out of the rodeo arena.

"So when do you plan to speak with Cathy White River about her gold panning?" Joe said.

"Maybe tonight," Frank said.

"Tonight?" Joe said in surprise.

"You heard what Pressel said," Frank said. "Everyone's invited to the big barbecue. I guess that would include us."

Joe wasn't sure what had made Frank change his mind about staying in Deadwood. Maybe he was as curious as Joe was about what was going on between Dan White River and John Pressel. Maybe he didn't want to leave without speaking to Cathy White River. Whatever it was, Joe wasn't going to ask. It meant they were staying another night. And they were going to attend a real western cookout. He could almost taste the food.

Frank and Joe returned to their campsite, washed up, changed into clean jeans and shirts, and by early evening were back in Deadwood, at the picnic grounds. The park was prettier than Joe had expected. It was a large grassy field, cut in half by a tiny stream. Trees had been planted to provide shade. Large barbecue cookers stood off to one side, where several chefs were almost completely hidden behind the smoke of the cooking meat.

Tables nearby held heaping servings of steaks, hamburgers, salads, corn on the cob, and homemade breads and desserts. Beyond the picnic area, a minicarnival had been set up, with a ring toss, a basketball throw, and a shooting gallery. A mechanical bull was attracting a large crowd. There were also booths where artists displayed leather work, jewelry, and native clothing.

Joe and Frank headed straight for the food tables. They each filled a plate with ribs, salad, and fresh rolls. Carrying their plates, they strolled through the picnic grounds.

A large banner was strung between two trees. Coming Soon—Deadwood Days! it proclaimed.

"John Pressel sure doesn't miss a promotional opportunity," Frank said. "I—"

"Excuse me," a female voice said from behind him. Frank turned to see Cathy White River. She was wearing a clean pair of jeans and a Black Hills State T-shirt. Standing beside her was Dan White River, a bandage over his left eye. "I didn't get a chance to thank you earlier," Cathy said hesitantly.

"That's okay," Frank said, surprised. "Hello."

"A lot happened very quickly this afternoon," Cathy's father said. "My daughter tells me you two young men helped her fight off a bully. And then you helped me fight one. To help a friend is one thing. To help a stranger is special. My thanks."

"We were glad to help, sir," Joe said. "We've had to learn to think on our feet in our detective work."

"Detective work?" White River repeated skeptically.

"Our father's a private detective in the East," Frank explained. "Sometimes we help him with his cases."

"We're pretty good at it, actually," Joe couldn't help adding.

"You certainly helped us today," Cathy said seriously. "No one else seemed eager to break up that fight."

"I'm sure Mr. White River could have taken

care of Slim by himself," Frank protested. "We just thought we'd speed things up a little."

"Hmm—you boys are modest, too," the older man said with a smile. He gently touched his bandaged area. "It certainly could have been worse. Please tell me your names so I can thank you properly."

"Frank Hardy, sir," Frank said, shaking hands with White River. "And my brother, Joe."

"Dad, Frank is the one who saw me panning for gold yesterday in the forest," Cathy said.

Frank's eyebrows shot up in surprise at Cathy's admission. He hadn't expected her to bring up yesterday's encounter. Cathy turned to him and added, "You have a right to know what I was doing up there—"

"Everybody having a good time?" a familiar voice boomed. John Pressel, who had changed into an all-white western suit, black string tie, and gray Stetson hat, approached the group. He was puffing on a thick cigar.

"We *were,*" White River said. Pressel chuckled, apparently taking the remark as a friendly joke. "I see you didn't come out of that scrape too badly, Dan," Pressel said, staring at the bandage. "Looks like young Slim got the worst of it. I ran into his buddies Rob and Doug a minute ago. They said he wouldn't be here tonight."

"That's too bad," Joe said. "We were looking forward to seeing Slim again before we moved on tomorrow." Pressel looked at Joe and Frank. "You two young fellas got into the action this afternoon, didn't you?" he said, a broad smile spreading across his red face.

"We're having a conversation here, Pressel," White River said. "Is there anything special you wanted to ask?"

"There is, Dan," Pressel said easily. "The financial group that's funding the theme park needs to submit a final budget plan to the zoning board by week's end. I just wanted you to know you have a few more days to reconsider your—"

"I'm not reconsidering anything, Pressel!" White River said. "You've had my answer. The matter is closed." He turned his back on Pressel.

Pressel blew a large smoke ring into the air, and his expression became a little more serious. "Maybe. Maybe not. Enjoy the picnic." Pressel tipped his hat to the group and walked off. White River turned to his daughter. "Cathy, I'm a little tired. I'm heading home."

"Okay, Dad," Cathy said. She turned to the Hardys. "I'm sorry, I'm going to have to leave—"

"No, no," her father said. "Why don't you spend some more time with these boys? They're guests in this town, after all." He turned to Frank. "Would you be able to give

47

my daughter a lift back to the reservation later? We came together."

"Of course," Frank said quickly.

"Do you feel up to driving, Dad?" Cathy asked.

"I'm fine, just a little bump on my head. I could drive these hills in my sleep. Don't worry about me." White River turned to the Hardys. "I hope we meet again soon. And again, my thanks. Not everyone risks his own safety to help a stranger."

"We'll get Cathy back safely," Joe said. The older man shook hands with Frank and Joe, kissed Cathy on the forehead, and headed off.

"I guess it'd be fair to say your father and Pressel aren't members of each other's fan clubs," Frank said once Cathy and the Hardys were alone.

Cathy ran a hand through her short, thick hair. "You've got that right," she said with a laugh. Then she added more seriously, "It's a long story—one that has to do with land and money. It's also why I was panning on federal land yesterday."

Frank shrugged. "It's probably none of my business. I figure you had good reason to do what you were doing." Frank had been thinking about Murph's comment that Cathy was majoring in mineralogy at Black Hills State. He doubted Cathy's panning had to do with personal profit.

48

Cathy smiled gratefully at Frank. She seemed relieved not to have to talk about the panning for the moment. "Well—anyone up for an ice-cream cone?" she asked brightly. The three of them wandered off, first to get ice cream, then over to the games area. As soon as Joe spotted the mechanical bull, he cried, "I've got to try that thing!" Frank held out his hand. "Be my guest."

For the next ten minutes Frank and Cathy watched Joe try to stay on the bull. After three turns Joe gave up—his back and his pride wounded a little. The three then walked over to the archery booth, only to watch Frank miss the bull's-eye target five times in a row. Cathy seemed to be having the best time of the three, entertained by the Hardys' dismal but funny attempts.

By now it had gotten quite dark. Though crowds still milled about, with Pressel shaking hands and slapping backs as enthusiastically as before, Cathy and the Hardys decided to call it a night. They climbed in the Hardys' black van, with Frank at the wheel, Cathy up front, and Joe in the backseat, and began the twisting, winding drive to the reservation.

"You know, if I were voting, you would have won the all-around award today," Joe said to Cathy. Frank smiled. It was clear that Joe liked this smart, talented, good-natured young woman. "The way you signaled to your horse alone should have won it for you."

"Thanks, Joe," Cathy said. "Those hand signals are just something I picked up as a kid on the reservation. I was able to get my horse to recognize them, and I guess it does impress people. But it's really very easy."

"It sure impressed me," Joe said. "How does your boyfriend feel about your roping calves—"

Suddenly the van lurched forward as Frank slammed on the brakes. "What gives?" Joe asked.

He peered out the front window to see several sheriff's cars and a Forest Patrol car with flashing lights on the right shoulder of the road. An ambulance was parked next to them, its back doors open. Flares lit the dark road.

"Must be some kind of accident," Frank said. He slowed the van to a crawl, and Joe and Cathy stared out the passenger window.

"Look!" Joe said. "A tow truck is pulling something out of the ravine."

Cathy pressed her face against the window. Then she let out a sharp cry. "No—no!" She screamed.

"What is it?" Frank said.

Cathy's choked voice could barely be heard. "That's my father's truck!"

Chapter
6

AFTER FRANK PULLED UP behind one of the patrol cars, Cathy White River jumped from the van and ran to the tow truck. Frank and Joe stepped onto the dirt shoulder of the road, which was filled with sheriff's officers. Frank saw the Forest Patrol's Sergeant Drake talking on a portable phone.

The Hardys walked over to Cathy, who stood watching the tow truck slowly pull a smashed white pickup back up onto the shoulder of the road. A sheriff's officer came over. "There's been an accident," he said. "I'm going to have to ask you to leave."

Frank turned to the officer and said quietly, "Her father was driving that truck."

"Oh, I'm sorry," the officer said to Cathy.

51

"Come over here and sit down. They've got him out and are moving him to the ambulance—"

"Daddy!" Cathy screamed, running over to the ambulance. The body of Dan White River had been lifted from the wreck and was being carried by stretcher to the ambulance. Frank watched a medic from the ambulance run to one of the emergency technicians carrying the stretcher and look at him questioningly. The technician shook his head and indicated for his partner to cover the body with a sheet. Cathy staggered toward the stretcher that bore her father's body.

"Oh, no," she said softly.

The technician raised his eyes. "Did you know the driver?" he asked her.

In a choking voice, Cathy murmured, "He's my father."

The technicians lifted the stretcher into the rear of the ambulance. "I'm sorry," he said. "He suffered a massive concussion. He never had a chance."

Frank and Joe came up behind Cathy, who had begun to tremble. "B-but, I was just with him a little while ago. He was fine. How could this have happened?"

Sergeant Burns of the Forest Patrol approached Frank, Joe, and Cathy. "I'm sorry, Miss White River," he said. "If you feel up to it, I'd like to ask you a few questions."

Frank whispered to Joe, "You stay with Cathy. I want to get a closer look at the truck." Joe nodded, and Frank went off.

The tow truck had now pulled the wrecked pickup onto the shoulder. Two sheriff's officers were inspecting it. Its front end was badly smashed where it had collided with a mass of boulders in the ravine. The entire windshield was gone. Frank noticed Sergeant Drake, Burns's partner, inspecting the rear of the truck.

"Sergeant Drake," Frank said.

"Frank Hardy. What are you doing out here?"

Frank quickly explained how he and Joe had met Cathy and her father at the picnic. Drake nodded grimly. "So the girl knows?"

"She's by the ambulance," Frank replied. "This couldn't have happened more than forty-five minutes ago, sir. How did the sheriff's office, the Forest Patrol, an ambulance, and a tow truck all get out here so fast?"

"The tow truck passed by just after the accident," Drake explained impatiently. "The driver radioed in the report, and we were able to be on the scene in minutes. Unfortunately, not in time to save White River."

Frank turned as the door to the tow truck opened. He almost gasped in surprise. Slim Davenport hopped down from the driver's seat.

"That's Slim Davenport!" Frank cried.

"Yep," Drake replied. "Slim's one of the best grease monkeys in the Hills." Frank stared as Slim stood by his tow truck, wiping dirt from his hands with a rag. Very convenient, Frank thought. Dan White River's truck "inexplicably" goes into a ravine, and Slim, who had a fight with him earlier in the day, happens to be driving by right after it happens.

Slim was talking now to two sheriff's officers. He pointed toward the mangled front right section of White River's truck. "There's your problem," Slim said. "Front left tire blew. Guy lost control and slid off the road. His tough luck he got stopped by a boulder." The officers bent down and inspected the front left tire. Frank walked over to Slim.

"You know who was driving that truck?" Frank demanded.

Slim turned and stared at Frank. "Well, well," he said. "I thought you'd be halfway to Pennsylvania by now."

"Dan White River, that's who," Frank said, ignoring his comment. "And he's dead."

Slim started to wipe his hands again. He stared at Frank. "That's too bad," Slim said. "Never like to see anybody go this way."

"Sergeant Drake said you were driving by here and accidentally came upon the accident," Frank said. "What were you doing driving a tow truck through the Hills at night?"

Slim stopped wiping his hands. He stared at Frank. "I don't have to answer any questions from a wise-guy tourist," he said. "But for your information, I was delivering some battery replacements to a customer up in Spearfish. Some of us got to work for a living. Some of us don't get spring break vacations." Slim turned back to the cab of the tow truck.

"I don't believe I caught the name of that customer in Spearfish," Frank said.

Slim spun around and glared at Frank. "Maybe because it's none of your business," Slim said. He tossed the dirty rag down on the ground and jumped into the truck cab.

Frank headed back toward the ambulance. Joe was talking softly with Cathy, who was seated on the ground, leaning against one of the sheriff's cars. Joe saw Frank and came over. "She's obviously in shock, but I think she's holding up pretty well," Joe said. "Since it was a death caused by unnatural causes, a patrol officer told me the body will have to be taken to Deadwood and held until tomorrow," Joe added.

"Coroner's report?" Frank asked. Joe nodded.

"You'll never guess who just happened to be driving by in his tow truck and was the first one on the accident scene," Frank said in a low voice. Just then an engine started up. Frank peered over and saw Slim's tow truck moving back onto the road, Dan White River's truck hitched to its rear.

"Well, I guess that explains why we didn't see him at the picnic," Joe said. "What was he doing out here?"

"He says he was on a delivery job," Frank said. Just then the ambulance carrying Chief Dan's body started up. Cathy came over to the Hardys. "I'm going with my father's body into Deadwood," she said, barely above a whisper. "The sheriff's department will give me a ride back to the reservation later."

"Cathy, if there's anything we can do—" Frank started.

Cathy held up a hand. "What is there to do?" she asked, her eyes starting to tear.

Frank put an arm around her shoulders. "We'll be staying over in case you need us tomorrow—"

"Tomorrow my father's body will be back on the reservation. People will be paying their respects. If you want to come . . ." she said, her quivering voice trailing off.

"We'll be there," Joe said. Cathy gave them a weak smile and stepped into the rear of the ambulance. The door closed and it took off.

The Hardys watched the ambulance disappear before heading toward the two Forest Patrol officers. "Maybe Burns and Drake can fill us in on some details," he said to Joe.

The Hardys approached Sergeant Drake,

who was making notes in a pad. Frank said, "Excuse me, Sergeant. Where is Mr. White River's truck being taken?"

Drake put his pencil away and said slowly, "Slim's taking it back to the garage. He'll give the vehicle a thorough inspection. It's routine in cases like this. We need to find out if human or mechanical error caused the accident."

"Is it routine to have a suspect inspect the evidence?" Frank asked, somewhat surprised.

"Evidence? Suspect?" Burns asked, puzzled. "Has a crime been committed here?"

"I heard that a blown tire caused the crash," Frank said. "Lots of things can cause tires to blow—some accidental and some intentional. Slim had a public brawl with Mr. White River today. He was also the first person at the accident site."

Drake glanced over at Burns and smiled. "Looks like we got ourselves a detective here, Burns. So, you think we could be talking murder?"

"Maybe," Frank said. "At any rate, Slim had the motive, opportunity, and means to cause Mr. White River's crash. I just think it's a little strange that he can drive off with the evidence."

"Well, thank you, son," Drake said, his face expressionless. "We'll try to do our jobs, and if anything comes up, we'll be sure to let you know. Is that okay with you?"

Drake nodded to Burns, and the two headed back to their car. The sheriff's officers were getting back into their cars as well. Engines started up, the cars pulled out, and soon Frank and Joe were standing alone on the shoulder of the dark, hilly road.

"Did you happen to notice the name on the side of Slim's tow truck?" Frank asked.

"Ace Mechanics, 785 Main Street, Deadwood, South Dakota," Joe replied instantly.

Frank smiled. "Good work. I think I'd like to get a closer look at that 'blown' tire—while it's still available."

Frank and Joe got back into their van and made good time back to Deadwood. Soon they were on Main Street, where tourists still mingled in small groups. As always there was a long line waiting to get into Saloon #10. Frank and Joe found Ace Mechanics about a block from Murph's Place, on the other side of Main Street. Frank pulled the van about a half block away and parked.

The Hardys approached the auto shop carefully. Both the garage, with its large driveway in front, and the small office adjoining the garage, were dark. Parked in the front driveway was the green van Slim had been driving the previous day. Next to it was the tow truck. The wrecked white truck had already been detached. "That was quick," Joe said. "Looks like nobody's home."

Frank approached the garage door and looked in the window. He could see the smashed truck up on lifts in the middle of the garage. Grabbing the garage door handles, Frank heaved upward. But the locked door wouldn't budge.

"Frank, over here!" Joe called out in a sharp whisper.

Joe was pointing at a window in the small auto shop office. It was open a crack. Joe quietly pushed the window farther up and, with a boost from Frank, hopped into the office. A moment later he opened the office door and let Frank in. Frank closed the door behind them.

Using the faint light coming through the garage windows from the streetlights outside, Frank and Joe approached the lift. In the silence of the cool, oily-smelling garage, they slowly walked around the battered metal that was once Dan White Feather's truck.

They both ended up staring at the left front tire, or what was left of it. The rubber hung in jagged strips from the wheel. It looked like an entire section had been blown away, leaving the remainder shredded to pieces. "Wow," Joe said. "This doesn't look like a simple blowout. It looks like the tire exploded."

Joe looked at Frank, who nodded. "A bullet," they said at the same time.

"Only a bullet would make a tire shred like this," Frank added. He stepped closer to the tire and squinted at the rubber through the darkness.

A scraping noise made Frank and Joe freeze.

The noise seemed to come from the office. Joe grabbed Frank's shoulder, and they both dropped to a crouch, out of the light from the window.

Joe heard soft footsteps enter the garage. Someone was approaching the truck.

In the dim light, Joe could see Frank turning his head, searching for a place to hide. Frank pointed to a movable tool cart about ten feet away. Joe gave a single nod and silently followed his brother toward the cart.

An instant later Joe felt a brush of air over his head.

He raised his head to see a shadowy figure standing over him. In the figure's hand was a crowbar, poised to strike.

Chapter
7

"HEY!" JOE CRIED OUT. Rising suddenly, he lunged for his attacker's legs and knocked him to the cement floor. The crowbar clattered to the ground.

At that moment the lights in the garage blinked on. Joe looked at the man whose legs he was holding. It was Slim Davenport.

"Slim!" he said, not at all surprised. The young man wriggled out of Joe's grip. At the same time, Doug and Rob ran into the garage.

"Doug," Slim said, standing up, "call the sheriff's office and tell them we caught two guys breaking and entering. Rob, check and see if anything's missing—"

"Hold it!" Frank called out. He and Joe jumped to their feet. "We came in here looking for you, Slim."

Slim laughed sarcastically, wedging a toothpick in his mouth. "Hiding out in the dark? Did you want to rob me or jump me? Oh, or maybe," Slim said, a fake look of shock on his face, "you wanted to check out old White River's wreck." He turned to Doug and Rob. "I knew I hadn't left the office window open all the way."

"You've got this all wrong," Frank said, smiling easily at Slim. "We're heading home tomorrow, and I wanted you to check out our van before we started off."

"You expect me to believe that?" Slim asked, spitting the words out so hard his toothpick flew from his mouth.

"This is an auto shop, isn't it?" Frank said innocently. "Why else would we come here?"

"You're lying!" Slim said. "And if you touched that wreck, that's tampering with official state property."

"We didn't touch the truck, Slim," Joe spoke up. "But we couldn't help noticing that front tire. It looks like it might have been shot."

"You're a pretty good shot, aren't you, Slim?" Frank asked.

Doug had paused at the door to the office. "Slim, you want me to call the sheriff or not?"

Slim spit onto the dirty garage floor. "No. These buzzards are leaving. And tomorrow morning they're leaving Deadwood." He glared at Frank. "Isn't that right?"

Frank turned to his brother. "Joe, I don't think Slim wants our business."

"Then I think we should go," Joe said. The Hardys moved toward the office door where Doug and Rob stood, blocking the doorway. Frank smiled at them. "Pleasure talking with you guys," he said as he and Joe squeezed past them.

As they were about to walk out, Frank turned back. "By the way, Slim," he said. "What was the name of that customer? The one you were delivering the battery to in Spearfish?"

"None of your business!" Slim shouted back. "You two had better leave while you still can!"

"Quick thinking," Joe said when they were on the sidewalk. "The bit about wanting to get the van checked out."

"Slim knew we were lying, but that's okay," Frank said. "We've got him worried, and that's what I wanted. It's pretty clear someone shot that tire. I'd like to get back into that office and check their records. I'll bet there was no business call tonight, in Spearfish or any-where else."

"That would mean staying over longer in the Black Hills," Joe said.

"I know," Frank replied. "But we're going to pay our respects to Cathy and her family tomorrow, anyway. Besides, Mr. White River deserves a little justice. From what I've seen so far, he's not going to get any around here." Frank yawned and added, "First, though, let's get back to camp. I think tomorrow's going to be a full day."

After a good night's sleep in the open air, the Hardys woke early the next morning. They showered and made the short trip back into Deadwood. Signs on Main Street informed them that there would be an Old West fashion show on Main Street at noon and a square dance that evening. A banner overhead reminded everyone of the reenactment of Custer's Last Stand, which would be the final event.

"Where to first?" Joe asked. He glanced over at Ace Mechanics, which was open for business. Several people stood in the driveway, although Slim and his pals weren't in sight. "You said you wanted to check the records in Slim's office. Looks like it's a little busy right now."

"It can wait," Frank said. "Let's get some breakfast. I think I know someone who might be able to help us." They headed toward Murph's Place.

The restaurant was busy, but Joe and Frank found seats at the counter. Between trips to the kitchen, Murph managed to answer the Hardys' questions.

"If it's official records or documents you want, then go to Town Hall," Murph told Frank. "Second floor, ask for Mr. Carter."

"Where would we go to check on a coroner's report?" Frank asked. Murph stared at Frank. "What exactly are you fellas up to?" he asked.

"Dan White River died last night," Joe said quietly.

"Yes, I heard," Murph said, shaking his head. "He was a good man. He's going to be missed."

"Not by everyone," Joe said.

Murph looked at Joe sharply. "Look, fellas, I'm not sure what you're thinking. But you're just passing through these parts. There's a lot of stuff going on here that you don't know anything about. Some of it goes back over a hundred years. Maybe you'd best leave well enough alone."

"We appreciate the concern, sir," Frank said. "We're just doing a little research, that's all."

Murph stared at the Hardys for a moment or two. "The sheriff's office, about four blocks down on Main, will be where you'll find autopsy and accident reports."

"Who said anything about accident reports?" Frank asked.

Murph returned his gaze. "I heard how Dan died. I figured you'd be interested."

"Thanks," Frank said. Murph gave him a weak smile and moved off toward some other customers.

"I'll check out Town Hall," Frank said. "Why don't you visit the sheriff's office?" They agreed to meet in an hour. After finishing their pancakes, sausages, and cornbread, they gave Murph a wave, left some money on the table, and set off.

A short while later Frank was standing in front of Deadwood's Town Hall. With its red-brick facade and two white pillars, it seemed to be from a bygone era. At three stories, it was one of the tallest buildings in Deadwood.

Inside, the hall was as quiet as a library. Only two people were seated at the long tables behind the information desk. A small, elderly man in a brown suit sat directly behind the desk. He was reading the *Deadwood Daily*. Frank noted that the front page had a picture of Mr. White River and the story of his death.

"Excuse me, Mr. Carter?" Frank asked.

The man lowered the newspaper an inch and stared at Frank over a pair of wire-rimmed glasses. "What can I do for you?" he asked in a soft voice.

"I'm looking for copies of all old treaties related to the Black Hills," Frank said.

Mr. Carter lowered the paper more to study

Frank. "What do you want with treaties?" he asked.

"I'm doing some research on the town for a school paper. Extra credit," Frank replied with a confident smile.

Carter nodded. "Against the wall, third row. Be careful, they break easy."

"Thanks," Frank said, heading for the wall.

"That's a joke," Carter called out after him. "See, they're always breaking treaties around here." Frank glanced back at Carter, but the old man was now reading his newspaper again. Frank reached the third row. There were dozens of racks, each containing oversize copies of the treaties. Frank pulled up a chair and got to work.

Meanwhile, Joe was entering the sheriff's office. In addition to the desk sergeant, two officers sat at small desks behind the large reception area. No one glanced up at Joe.

Joe was about to approach the sergeant when Forest Patrol Sergeant Drake entered behind him. Drake was clearly in a hurry. He marched up to the reception desk, not even noticing Joe.

Joe quickly stepped into a phone booth near the front door. He didn't feel like explaining why he was there to Drake. He'd just wait until the man left.

"Morning, Reynolds," Joe heard Drake say

to the desk officer. Joe peeked around the phone booth to see the two men.

"Hey, morning, Drake. What can we do for the Forest Patrol today?"

"I was wondering if you'd gotten the report yet on Dan White River."

Joe's ears perked up. Maybe Sergeant Drake had more interest in the accident than he'd let on the night before.

"Yeah, it came in about twenty minutes ago," Reynolds said, holding up a manila file.

"Does it reach any conclusions?" Drake asked.

"Accident was caused by a blown left tire," Reynolds said, glancing at the report. "It caused the driver to lose control of the vehicle, which then ran off the road and slammed into a boulder."

"What about the cause of the blown tire?" Drake asked.

Reynolds scanned the report. "Inconclusive. Says it could have been a defect in the tire, or the driver may have hit something on the road, or—" Reynolds paused and looked up.

"Or what?" Drake asked.

"Or possibly caused by a gunshot."

"Really?" Drake said.

Reynolds looked back at the report. "Says that because the tire was damaged so thoroughly the true cause may never be known."

Drake nodded softly.

"That's how the report ends," Reynolds said. "Signed by Slim Davenport."

"Thanks, Reynolds," Drake said. "Catch you later."

Joe stood inside the phone booth until Drake walked out the front door. Then he stepped out, deep in thought. So Slim had reported that the tire could have been blown by a gunshot. Still, Joe noted, the cause was finally termed "inconclusive." If Slim *had* shot at the tire, he was covering himself. On the other hand, Drake seemed suspicious. Joe hoped he'd follow up on the gunshot possibility.

Frank had found his treaty. He sat at one of the long tables with a copy of an 1894 agreement between the U.S. government and the Black Cloud tribe spread out before him. The treaty guaranteed that the Black Cloud tribe could continue to live forever on the thirty-six square miles they still occupied at present in exchange for temporarily giving up several thousand acres of land for one hundred years. That land would be returned to the tribe at the end of the hundred years, the treaty continued, if no valuable minerals were discovered beneath its surface.

Gold, Frank realized with a frown. The local miners must have hoped to strike it rich on the tribe's land, and they didn't want to risk letting any of that gold go to the Sioux Nation. No gold must have been discovered, or else the land wouldn't be being returned to the tribe.

According to the treaty, the details of the land transfer were spelled out in a separate section.

Frank returned to Mr. Carter and asked him for the extra section. "That document isn't with us," Carter said.

"Does anybody have it?" Frank asked.

"Of course," Carter replied. "Mr. White River—or whoever's going to take over for him. And the owner of the land to be turned over."

"Who would that be?" Frank asked.

"John Pressel," Carter said.

Frank thanked Carter and headed out.

Frank met Joe at the parked van. Joe slid behind the wheel. "Let's get out to the reservation," Frank said. He explained what he had learned about the treaty, adding, "Now, a hundred years later, the tribe is still stuck with just thirty-six square miles. No wonder Mr. White River got so angry when Slim started waving around those theme park shares at the rodeo."

Joe nodded thoughtfully as he took off for the Black Cloud reservation. He told Frank about the accident report. "So you think White River's death has to do with this treaty?" Joe asked.

Frank shrugged. "Could be."

"What could Slim have to do with an old business agreement?" Joe asked.

"I don't know," Frank admitted. "But I can guess that in these parts, business often comes down to who owns the land with the gold."

"Gold?" Joe said. "How does gold fit in?"

"When I first saw Cathy White River, she was panning for gold," Frank said. "Maybe there was more to her panning than I thought at first."

"You suspect Cathy of something, too?" Joe asked, raising his eyebrows.

"No," Frank said. "But she might know a few things that she doesn't realize may help. That's what we're going to find out."

"Okay," Joe said, "but remember, she just lost her father."

"I know," Frank said. "And the reason for her father's death is starting to bother me more and more."

Within fifteen minutes the Hardys had descended from the lush green hills onto the flat, more barren plateau. At the entrance to the Black Cloud Reservation was a sign warning trespassers that this was private land and to stay off. Frank stopped the van near the sign. There were no houses in sight.

"Drive on a little farther," Joe suggested. "Maybe we'll see another sign."

Frank drove the van slowly along the flat

road. A dirt drive veered off to the right, but there was no street sign, so Frank continued going straight. A moment later a small cloud of smoke appeared in the distance.

"It's a motorcycle," Joe said, peering through the windshield. "Let's ask the driver if he knows where Cathy lives."

Frank stuck a hand out the window to signal the driver. The motorcycle came to a stop beside the van, and a young, long-haired man in jeans and a T-shirt removed his helmet.

"Can I help you?" he asked Frank.

"I'm Frank Hardy, and this is my brother, Joe," Frank said. "We're looking for Cathy White River."

The man's dark eyes narrowed. "Wait here," he said. "I'll go tell her you're here." The man slowly took off on his motorcycle down a dirt road to Frank's left, which was lined with half a dozen small houses. A few old cars were parked in front of them. Children played nearby and laughed and pointed as the motorcycle driver parked near them.

"Time to get dressed," Frank said, pulling a couple of ties out of the glove compartment. They'd agreed to wear ties with their sports shirts and jeans for the day. It was the least they could do to show respect for Mr. White River and his daughter, Frank thought as he knotted his red- and blue-striped tie.

Suddenly loud shouts broke the stillness.

Frank peered toward the house nearest to them. He could make out Cathy White River, dressed in a long black skirt and gray blouse, running around the side of a house and up to its front door. Banging her fists on the door, she screamed, "Harry Leeds, how could you do this? I hate you!"

The door flew open, and a young man in a light blue shirt and khaki pants stood in the doorway. He held a telephone receiver in one hand.

"Hey," Frank said. "Is that the guy who was talking with John Pressel at the rodeo yesterday?"

Cathy began hitting the man on the chest, yelling, "How could you!"

"Is she all right?" Joe said.

"It doesn't look like it," Frank said. "Let's go help."

Before either of the Hardys could jump from the van, Harry Leeds had dropped his phone to grab both of Cathy's arms. His face seemed to be contorted in anger as he swung Cathy around and slammed her against the side of the cabin.

Chapter

8

"HURRY!" FRANK YELLED. He and Joe sprang from the van, reaching the doorway after the motorcycle driver. Two other tribe members had also run to the cabin. Cathy was pinned against the side of the cabin, pain and anger showing on her face. Harry Leeds held her arms in a firm grip.

The motorcycle driver reached out, and Harry relaxed his grip.

"Let go of her!" Frank shouted.

"Frank! Joe!" Cathy cried. Harry turned to the Hardys, and Cathy jumped away to stand between Frank and Joe.

"Who are these guys?" Harry asked.

"They're friends," Cathy said as she glared at Harry. Though shaken a bit, she was still angry. "You couldn't even wait for my father's funeral, Harry?"

"What do you mean?" Harry replied.

Frank thought the handsome young man didn't look threatening now as he nervously ran a hand through his short, neatly cut black hair. He seemed disturbed by Cathy's anger.

"Don't play so innocent," Cathy said, her eyes narrowed. "I heard a tribal council meeting is planned for eleven o'clock. There could only be one reason—to elect you the new chairman!"

"I'm sorry, Cathy," Harry said. "I meant no disrespect. I didn't tell you because I didn't want to bother you at a time like this. I know how you must be feeling—"

"You can't know how I'm feeling. It wasn't your father who was killed last night!" Cathy shouted.

"Would you like to be left alone now?" Frank asked Cathy.

Harry looked at Frank, his intelligent dark eyes flashing. "Who are these new friends of yours, Cathy?" he asked.

"Frank and Joe Hardy," she said. "They're just passing through, heading back East. But they were kind to my dad. I asked them to visit today."

Cathy turned to Frank and Joe. "Come on. I want to show you something." Before leaving she whirled toward Harry suddenly. "And you know what, Harry? Go have your council meeting. My father's beyond being hurt—by you or anyone else."

Cathy led the Hardys down the dirt road, past the cluster of small wooden houses. "Where are we headed?" Frank asked.

"To see my father," Cathy said quietly. Her anger had subsided and she seemed almost subdued.

Frank glanced back. Harry Leeds and the others were watching them go. "Aren't they coming, too?" he asked.

"No," Cathy replied. A truck passed by, and she exchanged a solemn wave with the driver. "My father is being honored in the traditional way. The people who were closest to him go to pay their respects now, a few at a time and in private. The funeral will be in three days. Harry and his friends can attend that."

"Frank and I weren't exactly close to your father," Joe said.

Cathy looked at them. "I know. But my mother died giving birth to me, and I have no brothers or sisters. My two best friends in the tribe are far away at college. Besides, you offered him your help on the last day he was alive, so it would mean a lot to me if you came along."

"We're honored," Frank said.

After walking for half an hour, past several small clusters of houses and finally through empty, undeveloped land, Cathy and the Hardys reached a small cemetery to the side of the road. A short distance beyond it was a slight rise in the flat surface of the plateau. On top of the rise was a platform with Dan's body on top. Three tribe members—two middle-aged women and an older man—stood before it. One of the women was weeping, while her two companions gazed sadly at the ground.

Cathy exchanged soft words and hugs with the members of her family, then introduced them to Frank and Joe as her father's elder brother, younger sister, and sister-in-law. "This is where my father would have wanted to be," Cathy said to the Hardys in a trembling voice, indicating the platform. "Outside, under the sky, among the Black Hills. Since early times, our people have honored their dead this way."

Her voice broke, and Dan's brother, Sam White River, put a comforting arm around her. "Dan was a man who always placed his brothers before himself," Sam told the Hardys. "He knew this land was the most sacred possession we have. Next to his family, he loved the land the most." Sam paused, gazing at the mesas with their pale pink and orange colors. "His spirit is happy here."

Cathy wiped her eyes, blew her nose on the handkerchief Sam White River handed her, and nodded in agreement. Then she took a long eagle's feather from where it had been pinned beneath her belt and, moving past her two aunts, placed it under the platform beside bunches of wildflowers, photographs, and other personal tributes. With her back to the others, she bowed her head and murmured softly in a language the Hardys couldn't understand.

Frank watched somberly, feeling the sun beat down on his head. Then out of nowhere a cloud passed across the sun. For a few moments a gray shadow covered the mourners. Then, with a gust of wind, the cloud passed on. The sun shone brightly again. Cathy lifted her head to gaze at her father's casket. Then she turned and walked off.

Frank and Joe followed Cathy toward the wide expanse of the reservation. The flat, yellowish desert stretched for miles, ringed by higher plateaus.

Cathy stopped, gazing out at the land. "All that area over there is what is supposed to be returned to us," she said, pointing toward one of the mesas. "My father looked forward to getting it back. He was going to turn it into a giant nature park, so tourists could see how beautiful the land here used to be and what it could be again."

Sam White River came up behind them. "He was going to plant trees, create a small lake, and protect the local wildlife from hunters,"

Sam said. "Dan loved animals. Especially the buffalo."

"Yes," Cathy said, smiling a little. "Especially the buffalo."

"Then why don't you see that the park gets built, in his memory?" Joe asked.

"It's not that simple, Joe," she said. "Some people think my father was being old-fashioned with his nature park idea. They think there are better ways of getting money from that land. Now, with Dad gone, everything could change."

"Has this got anything to do with John Pressel's Deadwood Days theme park?" Frank asked. "And his offer to buy that land back from the tribe so he can build on it?"

Cathy looked at Frank. "You've been doing a little research," she said, raising one eyebrow. "You're right. There are plenty of people here who believe that selling the land back to Pressel would bring our tribe more money than a nature park ever could. And in a way, it's hard to blame them. They dream of all the jobs there could be, selling hot dogs and operating the rides."

She turned suddenly. "I have to get out of here. Why don't we go back to my house and have something to eat?"

"I'll go with you," Sam said. "Just let me say goodbye to Emily and Sue."

As Cathy and the Hardys started back down

the road, Joe said, "I hope you don't mind my asking, but where are all the tepees?"

"The what?" Cathy looked at him sharply, then laughed and shook her head. "I hate to disappoint you, Joe, but we haven't lived in tepees since we stopped following the buffalo herds, around 1870. We all live in regular old houses now. They're not fancy, but they don't blow away in storms, either."

Just then there was a faint exploding sound from off in the distance. The ground trembled slightly. "What was that?" Joe said, looking around. "Earthquake?"

"Dynamite," Cathy said, closing her eyes briefly. "Pressel's men are starting to clear away land for Deadwood Days. And they're within their rights, since technically the land still belongs to them! They set off dynamite four or five times a day. I'll never get used to the sound."

As Sam rejoined them and they passed the first houses, several people came up to offer Cathy and her uncle their sympathy. Frank noted that except for the occasional headband, the people were dressed like anyone in any other American town. Jeans and T-shirts were the most popular form of dress. When he commented on this, Sam nodded. "Jeans are practical. We're sure not about to go out and skin a buffalo for breeches. Our town probably isn't that much different from yours—except it's a lot poorer."

Frank saw what Sam meant. There was very little in the way of conveniences, let alone luxuries. "Some of us didn't even have indoor plumbing until the 1980s," Cathy told him. "And the only cars you see are used and beat up. Since gold was discovered in the Black Hills, we've been crowded into smaller and smaller pieces of desert so that riches could be mined."

When they reached Cathy's house, the Hardys followed Cathy and her uncle into the small wooden cabin and looked around. Inside were two easy chairs, a couch, a TV set, a desk with a typewriter on it, and a kitchen area in the corner.

"I sleep on the couch when I'm home from school," Cathy explained. She nodded toward an inner room. "My father's bedroom is in there. You see, being chairman of a Sioux tribe doesn't carry a lot of glamour."

"Over half our people live below the poverty line," Sam added. "Most of us have a hard time finding work. We get by with a few town jobs and government jobs and a powwow for the tourists now and then. Dan tried hard to help make things better."

Joe had gone over to the desk in a corner of the room. "What are these?" he asked, picking up several sheets of paper with drawings on them.

"Those were ideas for the nature park my father had drawn up," Cathy said.

"They're fantastic! Frank, come take a look at these."

"I'll get some refreshments," Cathy said. She headed for the refrigerator as Frank and Sam went to the desk. Frank could see why Joe had been impressed. The pencil sketches were obviously done by a skilled hand. They depicted an area of lush grassland and tall trees. There was a lake where families were sailing little boats and feeding ducks. Another page showed a herd of buffalo roaming freely as people took photos of them. There was also a sketch of a gift shop and museum.

"If your dad was so determined to build this nature park and he represented the tribe, why has Pressel started dynamiting the land?" Frank asked as Cathy brought some lemonade and cookies over to the table. "I know you said he was within his rights, but did he really believe he could get your father to change his mind?"

Cathy shrugged. "Pressel nearly always gets what he wants. Maybe he believed that once people on the reservation realized how many jobs would be available, they'd get rid of my dad and elect a new tribal chairman. Then he could buy back the land at practically any price he wanted."

Frank nodded thoughtfully. It sounded like Pressel had a good reason to want Dan White River out of the way. Could he have been the one who shot out the tire on White River's truck?

That didn't make sense, Frank realized immediately. Pressel had been at the barbecue long after White River had left. The Hardys had seen him themselves.

"Cathy, I have a confession to make," Frank said, taking a sip of lemonade. "I read a copy of your tribe's treaty in the town records this morning. There was supposed to have been an extra section that spelled out the specifics of the land transfer, but it was missing. I was told that Pressel has a copy of it and your father had another. Would you mind if I looked at that section?"

Cathy and Sam White River exchanged a quick glance. Sam nodded.

"He kept it in the top right drawer of his desk, I think," Cathy said. She pulled open the drawer, opened an old cardboard box inside, and lifted out a piece of parchment paper. "Here it is," she said. "The piece of paper all my father's dreams were based on."

"I'll take that now, Cathy," a voice said from the front door. They all turned. Standing in the open doorway was Harry Leeds, along with several other young men.

"Oh, no, you won't, Harry," Cathy said sharply. "The last thing my father would have wanted was for you to have this paper."

"That treaty belongs with the chairman of the Black Cloud tribal council," Harry said. "And as of ten minutes ago, that person is me."

Chapter

9

CATHY TOOK A STEP BACK, holding the document out of Harry's reach. "Get out of my house!" she cried.

"As soon as you turn that treaty over to me," the new chairman said calmly.

"You're breaking tribal law if you don't, Cathy," Sam White River said softly. "Your father wouldn't want you to do that."

"My father wouldn't want Harry Leeds replacing him as chairman, either," Cathy said evenly.

"What's in that treaty that's so important to you?" Frank asked.

Harry Leeds narrowed his gaze on Frank. "This is none of your business," he said coldly. "You're here only as a guest."

"Why don't you answer him, Harry?" Cathy demanded. "Why *is* this treaty so important to you?"

Harry shook his head and sighed. "It's no big secret," he said at last, unable to keep the irritation out of his voice. He looked at Frank and Joe, but he was really speaking to everyone in the room. "That treaty was signed nearly a hundred years ago, after gold was discovered in the Black Hills. In it, we agreed to give up our rights to several thousand acres of land for one hundred years, so that the local miners could search for gold, silver, or other valuable minerals there. If no minerals were found on the land during that time, we were promised that we could reclaim it."

"Were any minerals found?" Joe asked.

Harry glanced at Cathy. "No," he said. "The land is to be returned to us this year. The current owner wants to keep it, though, and has made our tribe a very generous offer."

"My father turned down that offer," Cathy added angrily.

"For what?" Harry snapped, losing patience. "So he could plant some trees and raise buffalo?"

"His nature park would have brought us tourist dollars and still preserved the land," Cathy protested.

Harry shook his head. "You know I respected your father, Cathy. All of us did. But he was behind the times. Our tribe needs cash—right now. Look at how our people are suffering! Don't you want to give us the chance to feed our old people and build schools and hire some nurses for the clinic?"

"Of course I do!" Cathy shouted. "But if we sell that land back to John Pressel, we'll have nothing! In five years the money will be gone, and we'll be begging Pressel to hire us to fry his hamburgers and operate his roller coasters."

She held the piece of paper close to her. "Now," she said, barely able to control the anger in her voice, "I'm asking you to leave my house."

Harry hesitated. Then he turned to Sam White River and said, "I'm sorry." To Cathy, he added, "I'm the tribe's chairman now, Cathy. Whatever our differences, I hope you feel you can come to me with any problems." He nodded at the Hardys, then walked out. His friends followed.

Shaking her head, Cathy sank into the nearest chair. "I don't get it. I've respected Harry all my life. He was one of the first of our tribe to go to college. Then he came back, talking about how he wanted to help the rest of the tribe. But all he seems to care about now is how much money we can make and how fast we can make it. My father wanted progress, too, but he warned about forgetting our past."

"Maybe you should talk with John Pressel yourself," Frank suggested.

Cathy frowned. "What would that accomplish?"

"Maybe with your father's death, Pressel will feel more like honoring his hopes and plans."

Cathy gave a short laugh. "You don't know John Pressel."

"No," Frank admitted. "But if he were ever going to make a compromise with you, this might be the time."

"But Harry's the chairman now," Joe said. "He's the one who'll be dealing with Pressel."

"That's why Cathy needs to see Pressel as soon as possible—before Leeds does," Frank said. He stood still, hesitating.

"What is it?" Cathy asked.

"Well, this is a time of mourning for you," Frank said. "I feel a little strange suggesting you drive into town and talk to—"

"My father's dream is what's at stake here, Frank," Cathy said. "It's too late to save his life, but maybe I can keep his dream alive."

Frank smiled, admiring Cathy's spirit.

Sam White River agreed to stay to greet any more relatives. After hugging him goodbye, Cathy followed the Hardys out the door.

As they walked toward the van, Frank and Joe noticed that many tribe members were gathered near a large tepee on the other side of the main road.

"I thought you no longer used tepees," Joe said.

"We just have that one," Cathy replied. "It's where the council talks over important matters and picks new leaders. It's sort of like our senate. They're probably all talking about the big election." She scowled. "There's Harry now."

Joe spotted the handsome young man, now stripped to his waist, walking away from the tepee.

"Where's he going?" Joe asked.

"To the sweat lodge, I guess," Cathy told him. "He'll carry out a purification ceremony to cleanse himself for his job as chairman. A sweat lodge is kind of like a sauna."

"How long will he stay in it?" Joe asked.

"Until he thinks he's given the people a good show," Cathy said bitterly.

In a few minutes Frank, Joe, and Cathy were in the van, headed toward Deadwood.

"Cathy," Frank began carefully, "we don't have any solid proof at this point, but Joe and I think your father's 'accident' might not have been an accident."

From the passenger seat, Cathy turned to look at Frank in the back. "You think someone deliberately caused him to crash?" she asked, her eyes growing wide.

"We think there's a good chance," Joe said. "We checked out the blown tire on your father's car. It wasn't a bump or rock that blew it. We think someone shot it."

Cathy stared out the front window, lost in thought. Finally she nodded and murmured, "It makes sense. He wasn't at the picnic after the rodeo. He could have been waiting for Dad out on the road."

Joe nodded. "That's what we were thinking. He *says* he was working. And he expects us to believe that he just happened to be driving by in his tow truck right after your father's tire blew."

"Wait a minute," Cathy said, turning sharply to Joe. "Which 'he' are we talking about?"

"Slim Davenport. Who else?" Joe said.

"Slim Davenport!" Cathy exclaimed. "What makes you think Slim would kill my father?"

Joe and Frank made eye contact in the rearview mirror. "Cathy, you were at the rodeo. You saw what Slim did after your father tore up his stock certificate," Frank said.

"Slim's a hothead, no question about it," Cathy told them. "But he gets mad about something and then it's forgotten a minute later. Slim wouldn't kill my father."

"Then who were you talking about?" Joe asked.

"The person who stood to gain the most from my father's death," Cathy said bitterly. "Harry Leeds!"

There was silence in the van. "Cathy, if what

you're thinking is true and we can prove it, it would be devastating for your tribe," Frank said at last.

"The last hundred years have prepared our tribe for almost anything," Cathy replied, her mouth set firmly. "If Harry committed murder, he should be punished for it."

"That's a big 'if,' " Frank reminded her. "I'm not ready to let Slim Davenport off the hook."

"But how are you going to prove any of this?" Cathy asked.

"I'm not sure—yet," Frank answered simply.

They arrived in Deadwood, and Joe found a parking place on Main Street. "Where can we find Pressel?" Frank asked.

Cathy pointed to a building across the street. "Probably at the bank."

"Okay," Frank said. "How about if Cathy and I try to get to see him? And then—"

Joe nodded. "I know—I'll wander over to Ace Mechanics to see if I can pick up a little information—like whether Slim Davenport really made a delivery to a customer last night."

Frank suggested they meet in half an hour. "How about meeting at Saloon Number Ten?" Joe asked. "I want to be able to say I had a hamburger in the place where Wild Bill Hickok played his last hand." Frank and Cathy agreed, and they set off for the bank.

Deadwood's bank was not particularly big. There were a few teller's windows, and a few customers were doing business there. Off to the far side of the bank was a metal railing and beyond that a closed door. A secretary sat at a desk outside the door. She was typing on a word processor. "That's Pressel's office," Cathy said. Frank and Cathy walked over to the secretary.

"May I help you?" the blond, middle-aged woman said, raising her head.

"We'd like to see Mr. Pressel," Frank said.

"Do you have an appointment?" the secretary asked.

"No, but you can let him know Cathy White River's here, and it concerns the Black Cloud treaty. He'll probably be interested."

The secretary stared at them. "Mr. Pressel's in a meeting, but if you have a seat I'll let him know you're waiting—"

A yell from within Pressel's office cut her off. "I want my stock!" the voice boomed. The door flew open so forcefully it banged against the adjoining wall. Slim Davenport, in his Ace Mechanics uniform, stood in the doorway, shouting at John Pressel. "I *won* that stock certificate! I can't help it if some crazy old man tore it up!"

Pressel shook his head. "I'm sorry, Slim. We can't replace the shares that easily. We will have to submit proof that your shares were destroyed. It's going to take some time before we'll be able to issue you new stock."

"Proof? What kind of proof?" Slim shouted. "The old man's dead! And I can't get back the ripped-up pieces of the stock certificate."

Pressel glanced at the outer office area. He saw Frank and Cathy watching them, along with all the other people in the bank. Pressel nodded toward Cathy. "Maybe someone else can help you."

Slim spun around. "You!" he shouted at Cathy. "You owe me!" Before Cathy could react, Slim leapt onto the metal railing and lunged for her.

Chapter
10

SLIM'S BRIEF PAUSE on the railing was all Frank needed. He pulled Cathy out of the way and watched Slim land in a heap on the carpeted bank floor. As Slim scrambled to his feet, Frank met him with a solid right to his midsection. Slim doubled over, then sprang back up and threw a punch of his own.

A bank guard ran over and jumped between Frank and Slim. Slim was still full of fire. "You're going to help me get back that stock!" he shouted at Cathy. "It was worth thousands of dollars. You'd better sign a notarized statement that it was your father who destroyed my stock!"

Frank shook his head. "A man's not dead

one day and you come running after his daughter. Have some respect."

Slim glared at Frank. "I thought you were leaving town."

"Not yet, Slim. I've got too much to do," Frank said.

"Well, this had better be the last time I see you," Slim said, pointing a finger at Frank's chest. "And as for you, I'll definitely be seeing you again," he said to Cathy. Slim then pushed his way past the bank guards, strode to the exit, and left. Pressel nodded to the guards, and they moved off. The bank customers who had gathered to watch the scuffle filtered away.

"Mr. Pressel, these young people wanted to see you about a treaty," the secretary said.

Pressel acted sympathetic toward Cathy. "My condolences, my dear. I heard about the tragedy. It's unbelievable."

"What's unbelievable is that you turned Slim Davenport loose on her a moment ago," Frank said.

"I'm sorry about that," Pressel said, his rosy face coloring to purple. "I didn't think—I was just desperate to get him out of my office."

"Never mind that," Cathy said. "Slim isn't what brought us here."

Pressel cleared his throat. "You mentioned the treaty. Why don't we go into my office?"

Pressel's office was elegant, especially in contrast to Cathy White River's reservation home, Frank thought. It was furnished with a thick rug, two plush couches, and a large mahogany desk. Pressel sat down behind the desk, and Frank and Cathy sat on one of the couches. Pressel took a cigar out of a gold box that had the initials *JP* on it. He lit the cigar and blew smoke toward Frank. "I'm afraid I've forgotten your name, young man," he said.

"Frank Hardy, sir."

Pressel stared at Frank through the cigar smoke. Finally he turned to Cathy. "My dear, your father and I had our disagreements at times. My lasting regret shall be that he went to his death at such a moment."

"Maybe you can do something about that regret," Cathy said. "I know what the major disagreement was about. My father refused to sell back the land that's being returned to our tribe before the end of the year."

"Yes—so what are you getting at?" Pressel asked, holding his cigar between his index finger and thumb.

"Cathy believes you're going to try to make a deal with the tribe's new chairman," Frank told him. "It's possible that he'll accept your money. But if you really want to honor the memory of Mr. White River, then you won't offer to buy that land."

"Have you been elected as a spokesperson for the Black Cloud tribe?" Pressel asked, sounding amused.

"Yes," Cathy said, annoyed.

Pressel nodded pleasantly. "Let me show you something." He turned to the wall directly behind his desk and pulled down a map that stretched from the ceiling almost to the floor. Frank saw that it was a detailed map of the plateau area, and the section of the Black Hills National Forest that bordered it.

"The land that's being returned to your tribe, Cathy, lies right next to this tract, which I own," Pressel said, pointing with a pen. "If I put the two together it will add up to just the right acreage to build Deadwood Days."

"Who owns the land on the other side of the plateau?" Frank asked.

"I do," Pressel said.

"Then why don't you just build in that direction?" Frank asked. "You'd still have all the room you need for your theme park and you wouldn't have to pay the Black Cloud tribe a penny."

Pressel nodded, as if he'd heard this argument before. "That land is too far from Deadwood," he explained. "Even if we put up a hotel next to the theme park, we'll still need Deadwood's support services—motels, restaurants, gas stations, and so on. According to our research, building the park more than forty miles away could reduce its profits as much as thirty percent. Anyway, the park is supposed to help boost Deadwood's tourist business. It won't help us much if it's that far away."

"It's not fair, Mr. Pressel," Cathy cut in, her voice low with anger. "Originally that land was taken from our tribe because the government believed they'd strike gold on it. Now that it's been proved worthless, it's about to be tossed back to us like leftovers. And at the last minute, when you've come up with a way to make a profit off it, you want to take it from us again."

"I'm not taking it, Cathy. I'm offering cash for it. A lot of cash." Pressel pulled on the map and it rolled back up. "Your dad had his reasons for not wanting to sell. But if the new chairman has different ideas—" Pressel held up his hands. "Business is business, right?"

"How much are you offering for the land?" Frank asked.

"Fifteen million," Pressel said coolly, puffing on the cigar.

"Father told me eighteen million," Cathy said, eyeing Pressel suspiciously.

Pressel coughed nervously and placed the cigar in an ashtray. "Whatever the price, it was an attractive offer. I frankly don't know how he could expect your tribe not to accept it."

"Maybe making a lot of money isn't as important to some people," Cathy said hotly. "Maybe some of us care more about the land."

"Mr. Pressel, I suggested Cathy come to see

you today because I thought you might be understanding at this time," Frank interjected.

"I am very understanding, kids," Pressel said. "Now you need to understand something. This area can't keep growing with two-bit gimmicks like Wild West Week to perk up the off-seasons. A theme park will bring in tourists year-round, and that means year-round jobs for the tribe as well. I'm sorry that we can't make much money off buffalo." He shook his head almost regretfully. "But in business you have to be practical. I've made an offer; the tribe has the right to refuse it. It's not my problem."

The intercom on Pressel's desk buzzed. "Yes?" Pressel said, pushing a button.

"Your lunch date's in half an hour, sir," the secretary's voice said through the speaker.

"Thank you," Pressel said, rising from his chair. Frank and Cathy stood up. "I've enjoyed our talk," Pressel said. "Feel free to drop by anytime. And, again, Cathy, my condolences."

"Thank you," Cathy said, drawing herself up. "But my father's death doesn't mean you win. It means it's my turn to fight."

Pressel shook his head. "I'm sorry you feel that way. We'll have to see how the rest of your tribe feels."

Frank took Cathy by the arm and the two of them headed for the door.

*   *   *

As Joe entered the tiny office of Ace Mechanics, Doug Pitman, wiping off the grease on his hands, appeared from the garage. "Yeah, what do you want?" he asked, eyeing Joe suspiciously.

"I need a window scraper," Joe said. Doug stared at him a moment. "Do you have any?" Joe asked, trying to sound impatient.

Doug gave a short jerk of his head. "Wait here. And don't touch anything."

Doug went back to the garage, and Joe quickly turned to the metal desk in the office. He shuffled through papers and auto parts books before he found what he was looking for—a date book.

Glancing nervously at the door to the garage, Joe turned to the previous day. At eight P.M. the name "Loudon" appeared, followed by the notation "deliv. batt." Joe assumed that meant delivery of a battery. So maybe Slim was telling the truth. Maybe he *had* been on a delivery run and just come across the accident. Or had he written that entry into the date book later to cover his tracks? Joe would have to see if there was anyone named Loudon in Spearfish.

A clank from the garage startled Joe, and he flipped the book shut. He looked up as Doug walked through the doorway with a long, thin box.

"Four seventy-five," he said.

"What?" Joe said.

"The windshield scraper. It costs four dollars and seventy-five cents."

"Oh," Joe said. He shook his head. "Never mind. They're only four twenty-five where I live. Thanks anyway, Doug." Joe headed for the door before Doug could say anything. As he left, he casually nodded toward the garage. "Where's the truck that was up there last night?"

"The Forest Patrol has it. They impound any car for thirty days following a fatal accident on park land. Is that okay with you?" Doug snarled.

"Fine," Joe said and walked out.

Several minutes later Joe walked into Saloon #10. Frank and Cathy were already seated at one of the old-fashioned tables. Fiddle and banjo music played in the background. The waiters were all dressed in western outfits and had handlebar mustaches.

"How'd you make out?" Frank asked Joe as he sat down. Joe described what he'd seen in the date book and suggested they check for a Loudon in Spearfish. A waiter came over and they all ordered burgers, fries, and large sodas. Then Frank and Cathy filled Joe in on their conversation with Pressel.

Cathy turned to the Hardys. "I want to tell you what I was doing when you saw me panning for gold," she said as their orders arrived. She waited for the waiter to leave before she continued. "Our treaty is very specific. It says the land will be returned to us only if no valuable minerals have been found within its boundaries.

"Well, the fact that the land's being returned to us would seem to indicate that there's nothing valuable left in it," Cathy said. "But my father was very suspicious. Why would John Pressel make him an offer of millions of dollars when he could just as easily build his theme park on the land on the other side of the plateau?"

"But Pressel just told us that the location of your land is better," Frank said.

"He told my father the same thing," Cathy said. "But my father didn't believe him. Dad believed that Pressel suspects there are still valuable minerals in the ground, but he's afraid the treaty will run out before he finds them. So Pressel is willing to pay a lot of money for the land now, hoping to find whatever might be there later. That's why I was panning up where you saw me. That stream runs down into the plateau. Dad thought it might be carrying gold into what would soon become our land."

"I see," Frank said, nodding. "If the land still contains valuable minerals, then Pressel can keep the rights to it. But if the treaty kicks in before he can find the minerals, then he loses the land. So he was offering to buy the land now hoping to strike it rich later."

"That's what my father thought," Cathy said, picking up her hamburger.

"Seems like an awful lot of money to spend on a hope," Joe commented.

"I agree," Cathy said. "That's why my dad was convinced Pressel knew something he wasn't telling anybody. He thought if we could find out what that something was, we'd be able to expose Pressel's whole theme park proposition as nothing more than a scam, a cover for his real intentions. If there really is gold on that land, it would be worth much more than a theme park and a nature park put together."

"When did Pressel first announce plans for the theme park?" Frank asked, biting into a french fry.

"Less than a year ago," Cathy said.

"Would he have to buy any special equipment to look for gold or other minerals?" Frank asked.

Cathy nodded. "He probably has it." Suddenly her eyes widened. "But it just occurred to me—if Pressel's been looking for precious metals, he's probably had ore samples tested at the assayer's office."

"Assayer's office? What's that?" Joe asked.

Cathy looked at him. "It's where prospectors go to find out whether they've struck it rich," she explained. "The assayer analyzes samples of ore that prospectors have dug out of the ground. If the ore contains a certain percentage of, say, gold or silver, the prospector can file a claim and start building a mine."

"Is there an assayer's office in Deadwood?" Frank asked.

"Are you kidding? Of course there is," Cathy replied. "A few blocks down from here."

"We'll check it out," Frank said. "In the meantime, now that your father's truck is with the Forest Patrol, we'll contact Drake and Burns to see if they'll let us check it out. We didn't get a very thorough look when it was at Ace Mechanics."

"But right now," Joe said with a grin, pushing away his plate, "I'm going to sit in the chair where Wild Bill Hickok got shot playing poker."

Cathy laughed. "You can't sit in the chair." She pointed toward a table near the front of the saloon. One of the chairs was suspended in midair, hanging by wires from the ceiling. "They have to keep people out of the chair or it would have broken years ago."

"I still want to see it up close," Joe said.

As soon as they had finished eating and paid the bill, the three of them headed over to the table. The chair hung three feet off the ground with its back to the door. "Just think," Joe said. "Wild Bill Hickok sat right here. And got shot here, too."

Frank glanced out the front window of the saloon onto Main Street. "Hey, isn't that John Pressel?" he said, pointing.

As Joe and Cathy turned around, Frank watched Pressel approach a man on the opposite sidewalk. He shook hands with the man, whose back was to them. The two began walking to the restaurant across the street, the Bull 'n' Bison.

"Guess that's Pressel's lunch date," Frank said. The man took a quick glance backward, and Cathy White River gasped.

"I can't believe it—that's Harry Leeds. There's only one reason why he'd have lunch with Pressel. He's going to sell our land to him today!"

Chapter

11

CATHY BOLTED for the door and ran out, Frank and Joe sprinting after her.

At the curb Frank grabbed Cathy by the arm. "Hold it!" he said.

Cathy turned on him angrily. "My father's not dead a day and Harry Leeds is meeting with the man who wants to take away our land. I'm not going to just stand here and watch the deal happen." She turned away, trying to twist out of Frank's grip.

"At least let me come with you," Frank said.

"Fine," Cathy said impatiently. "Let's go."

"Go ahead," Joe urged Frank. "I'll run over to the assayer's office and try to find out if Pressel's sent any samples there lately."

As soon as Joe got the words out of his

mouth, Cathy pulled Frank across the street to the Bull 'n' Bison.

Inside the restaurant, it was dark and quiet. Soft carpeting and heavy white tablecloths muffled most of the noise. There were only a few tables filled, but the people seated at them wore dresses and business suits.

A hostess gave Frank and Cathy a phony smile. "Two for lunch?" she asked doubtfully.

"No, thanks. I think I see my party," Frank said, glad that he was wearing a tie at least.

Frank and Cathy hurried into the dining room and immediately spotted Pressel and Harry Leeds in a booth in the rear. Cathy marched over to the table, with Frank following her.

"Well, I'm surprised you're not breaking out the champagne," Cathy said sarcastically. "You can't have a victory party without that."

"Cathy!" Leeds said in surprise. "Wh—what are you talking about?"

"Have you sold our land yet, or are the two of you just toasting my father's 'accidental' death?" Cathy went on bitterly.

"Cathy, please," Harry said quietly. "Your father's death was a terrible blow to all of us."

"So this is how you mourn? By meeting with Pressel as fast as you can?" Cathy said.

Leeds shook his head sadly. "Cathy, I've been having discussions with Mr. Pressel for the past several months. You know that not all of us agreed with your father's decision to turn down his offer to buy our land—"

"I wanted all of your people to know how big the offer was that your father was rejecting," Pressel interrupted. "It didn't seem fair that one man could keep that much money from your tribe."

"Spare me the political speeches," Cathy said. "Why don't both of you tell the truth, Harry—you want as much money as you can get as fast as you can get it."

"I don't want to exploit the land any more than you do," Harry said with conviction. "But I'm being realistic. It would take a lot of bank loans for the tribe to start a development project on its own. Where would that money come from?"

"And you're willing to sell us out so easily?" Cathy said, pleading with Leeds. "Harry, that land was stolen from us! And now you're going to lose it for us again!"

"So just because I don't like what happened a hundred years ago, I should make the next hundred years just as bad?" Harry retorted.

"Wise words, Harry," Pressel said. "We can't undo the past. But we can make the future better." Pressel took an envelope from his jacket pocket and pulled out two pages. "Now, do you think we could have a little privacy for our discussion?

Harry looked up at Cathy. "Cathy, you have

my word that I only want to do what's best for the tribe. Now I have to ask you to leave. If you don't, then I'll have to bring up your behavior at the next council meeting." Harry took one of the pages from Pressel. Pressel held the other, and the two men put their heads together and began to talk softly.

Cathy turned away from the table, tears in her eyes. Frank took her arm, and they began to walk from the dining room. Frank looked over his shoulder at the booth once more. Pressel had taken a gold-tipped pen from his inner pocket. The men were about to sign.

"Hold it!" Frank rushed back to the table. Pressel and Harry looked up.

"Frank, what are you doing?" Cathy said, following him.

"I didn't want to say anything before, but now I have no choice," Frank said. "My brother and I have been doing some investigating, and we believe that Dan White River's death wasn't an accident. We think he may have been murdered."

"That's a very serious charge, young man," Pressel said, frowning.

"You're right," Frank said. "And I wouldn't make it if I weren't serious. That's why I think if you two signed any agreement today it would be extremely suspicious—one day after Dan's accidental death."

Pressel and Leeds were silent. Pressel focused on the tablecloth while Harry turned to Cathy.

"Harry," Cathy said, "he's telling the truth. We really are onto some leads. If my dad's death wasn't an accident, then how will this look?"

Harry sighed, forcefully expelling all the air in his lungs.

"If the circumstances of Dan's death are suspicious, then by all means we should call for a thorough investigation," Pressel said impatiently. "Still, our deal was for thirteen million dollars for today and today only." Frank's eyebrows shot up. Pressel's offer was lower every time Frank heard it.

"Harry, what's the harm in waiting a few days?" Cathy pleaded. "Just until the real cause of my father's death is cleared up one way or the other?"

Harry looked up at Cathy. "Okay," he said finally. "I'll give you three days to prove your father was murdered. We meet back at this restaurant in seventy-two hours. Either you have proof for me then or I sign the agreement with Mr. Pressel."

Cathy smiled at him, relief flooding through her. "Thank you, Harry," she said quietly.

Pressel gathered the papers together and put them back in the envelope. "I accept your position, Harry. But as a businessman, I know that a lot can change in seventy-two hours. My offer won't be as generous in three days."

"What do you mean?" Harry asked.

Pressel stood up and adjusted his tie. "For each hour that passes without your signing this agreement, I'm reducing my offer by one hundred thousand dollars. I'm sorry, Harry. But this kind of delay could really hurt me. Good day, folks." He nodded to Frank and Cathy and walked out of the dining room.

Harry looked at Cathy and Frank, clearly troubled. "A hundred thousand dollars an hour. In seventy-two hours the deal will be worth less than half of what he's offering now."

"You're doing the right thing, Harry," Cathy said nervously.

"I hope so," Harry said. "Or we're going to have a lot of explaining to do back home."

"Pressel's already cheated you out of five million, Harry," Frank said. "He offered Mr. White River eighteen million. Then he told us it was fifteen. And now he's trying to make thirteen sound generous. The fact is, that land's probably worth a lot more."

"The fact is, you've already wasted one minute," Harry said. "And right now, time is money."

A short while later Frank and Cathy met Joe at the Hardys' van on Main Street. Frank described the outcome of their conversation with Pressel and Leeds. Then Joe told them about his trip to the assayer's office.

"I almost missed it," he said. "It's a tiny place, squeezed between a dentist's office and a greeting card shop."

"Did you find out anything?" Cathy asked impatiently.

"Of course. It took some work," Joe told her, not willing to make his job sound easy. "I figured those records are confidential, or anyone who heard about a successful test might rush to the land in question and stake a claim."

"So what did you do?" Frank asked.

Joe grinned. "I told the secretary I was Pressel's nephew visiting here to help my uncle dig for gold. The secretary was shocked. She said there'd never been any gold on Pressel's property, and that even if there were, he's so caught up in tearing up the land for his silly old theme park he wouldn't notice if it were made of gold." Joe glanced triumphantly at Cathy. "Sounds to me like we can rule out precious metals as Pressel's motive for buying back the land."

Frank nodded. "Well, we just told Pressel and Leeds that we think Mr. White River was murdered. So if one of them is behind his accident, chances are he'll be watching our every move."

Cathy shuddered. "Just thinking that Harry

might be responsible for my father's death gives me the creeps," she said.

"Pressel also stood to gain from your father's death," Frank reminded her.

"Pressel has an alibi, Frank," Joe reminded him. "He was at the picnic when the accident took place. We saw Harry and his friends leave much earlier—remember?"

"What we really need is solid evidence," Frank said. "Let's get a closer look at your father's truck, Cathy. It's at the Forest Patrol station. Where's that?"

"It's back in the Hills," Cathy said. "About three miles from where my father ran off the road."

"Let's go," Joe said. They got back into the van and Frank drove out of Deadwood. Soon they were climbing the winding Black Hills roads again.

"Maybe we can also take a ride up to Spearfish," Joe suggested. "See what we can learn from that customer of Slim Davenport's."

Frank nodded, his eyes on the road. He had just headed onto a level part of the highway when he raised his eyes to the rearview mirror and caught sight of a car approaching rapidly from behind. It was a green van. "Speaking of Slim," Frank said, indicating the green van, "I wonder where he's off to now."

All at once Frank noticed that the van's windows were tinted dark, making it impossible to see the driver.

As the green van came within a few yards of the Hardys' van, Frank saw that the tinted rear window of the green van was open a few inches. Then the green van picked up speed and started to pass the Hardys. From out of the open window the muzzle of a gun suddenly appeared. It was aimed in the direction of the Hardys' van.

"Hey—" Frank began.

He was cut off as the sound of gunshots exploded into the air.

Chapter

12

FRANK SWERVED SHARPLY to the right and skidded onto the shoulder of the road. Bullets pelted the dirt and gravel near the front tires. Then the green van sped past.

Cathy gasped. "They were trying to kill us!"

Frank's jaw was set firmly as he slowed the van. "No. They were aiming for the tires—so we'd lose control."

"They're getting away!" Joe shouted.

"No, they won't. Hold on!" Frank took off after the green van.

"Be careful!" Cathy cried as Frank guided the van around the highway's treacherous turns. He was just at the speed limit, but it was their only chance of catching their attacker. Frank decided he had to take that chance.

"I guess this proves that Slim is capable of shooting at people," Joe noted, a trace of excitement in his voice.

Cathy shook her head, her face pale. "I can't believe it," she said. "Slim Davenport killing my father? And now going after us? I've known Slim all my life. What could he possibly hope to gain?"

"Revenge," Frank said, "and profit." He took a sharp turn and nearly skidded off the road. He had lost sight of the van. "Your father ripped up Slim's stock certificate. Slim was angry—and afraid that if Deadwood Days was never built, he'd never get any profit from it. With one shot at your father's car, he got back at your father and got rid of the main opposition to Deadwood Days. Now that we've started to investigate, he can hardly afford to have us around, either."

"And it wasn't just Slim," Joe added "That gunshot came from a rear window. There had to be at least two people in the van."

"My guess is there were three," Frank said as he came around a sharp, blind turn.

"Look!" Joe yelled. "On the right." Sitting on the side of the road was the green van. Frank pulled over and parked right behind it. The three of them got out and cautiously approached the vehicle. All the windows were rolled up. The glass was tinted so dark that it was impossible to tell if anyone was still inside.

Frank tried the doors of the van. They were locked. Joe peered in through the dark windshield. "I don't see anyone," he said at last.

Frank touched the hood. "It's still warm. They must have ditched it and taken off across the hills," he said.

"There's another possibility," Joe said. "They could have had another car parked and waiting for them here. Then they could have driven back into town without anyone noticing."

"But how could they explain the green van ending up here near the reservation?" Frank asked. "And how could they know *where* we were going and where we'd be. Doesn't make sense to me. I think they just took off."

"They could claim the van was stolen." Joe had returned to the Hardys' black van and was inspecting the front. He bent closer toward the front left door.

"Hey—look what we have here," Joe said. He pointed to a small hole near the bottom of the door. "It looks like a bullet went through the door." He opened the door and lifted the mat under the driver's seat. "Here it is," he said a moment later, prying a small chunk of metal out of the padding beneath the mat. "Looks like Slim was using a .45."

"Good eye," Frank said. "I say we drive on to the Forest Patrol station. We can call the sheriff's office from there and report the shooting. And maybe we can find out if this bullet matches anything they may have found on Mr. White River's truck."

Suddenly the squeal of tires and the loud roar of an engine cut through the silence. Frank looked up to see the Ace Mechanics tow truck barreling around a curve in the highway. Slim Davenport was at the wheel with Rob Mitchell next to him.

The tow truck pulled up behind the Hardys' van and came to a screeching halt. Slim and Rob jumped from the cab. "I knew it!" he yelled. "Breaking into my garage wasn't enough, huh? Now you steal my van!"

"You must think we're pretty stupid," Joe said, taking a step toward Slim and Rob.

"No," Slim said. "I know you are." He pulled a gun out from inside his jacket. "You two think you can get away with anything, don't you? Well, not this time. Stealing a van is a serious crime," he said in mock disapproval.

Cathy stepped up to speak to Slim, but before she could get a word out, the wail of a siren filled the air. Frank saw a Forest Patrol car come roaring around the bend. It was number 333. The car pulled to the shoulder and slammed to a stop in a cloud of dust. Sergeants Drake and Burns got out quickly.

"What's going on here?" Burns asked. "Give me that gun, Slim. Now!"

Slim handed the .45 to the Forest Patrol officer. Meanwhile, Drake slowly removed his sunglasses and turned his steely gaze on Frank and Joe. "So we meet again. What's the story this time?" he demanded.

"I'll tell you the story," Joe said quickly. "These two tried to shoot out our tires while we were on our way to see you. We chased them, but they pulled away from us. We found their van parked here, where they must have ditched it. Their tow truck must have been hidden nearby. Then they came racing back in the tow truck and caught us here, and now Slim's trying to accuse us of stealing his van!"

"They *did* steal it, Sergeant!" Slim protested. "I looked out my garage window about half an hour ago and saw somebody jump into my van and drive away! Rob and I took after them in the truck. We kept circling through the hills, but we couldn't find them. Then we come upon this crew here. We caught them red-handed!"

"We weren't anywhere near your garage," Frank retorted. "As Joe said, we were on our way to Forest Patrol headquarters to see if there were any clues to Cathy's father's death that might have been found on his truck. That is, assuming you didn't destroy all the evidence already."

"I didn't touch that truck!" Slim yelled. "And I didn't shoot at it either."

"Oh, you just thought it was such a good

idea that you tried it on us," Joe said wryly. "But this time you made one mistake." He held up the bullet. "You left behind a major piece of evidence."

"Let me see that," Drake said, taking the bullet from Joe. Turning it over in his hand, he examined it closely. "Someone shot this at your van?" he asked. In answer, Joe pointed to the hole in the van's door. Drake looked at Burns and then back at the bullet. Finally, he turned to Slim.

"Come with me, son," he said firmly.

"I don't have to do anything," Slim said, turning his anger on Drake. "These guys are lying."

Drake's eyes flashed, and he motioned for Burns to stand near Slim.

"We've just been talking to the sheriff's office," Drake began slowly. "The lab technicians over there just finished testing the shredded tire from Dan White River's truck. They gave us some very interesting information." The group grew silent as they stood on the side of the windy highway.

Drake stared at Slim, unblinking. "The sheriff's office has reached two conclusions. One, they believe someone altered the left front tire and front hood area after the accident. And one of the few people with access to the truck after the accident was you, Slim." Slim started to speak, but Drake held up his hand.

"Two, the technicians found fragments of what they believe was a .45 magnum bullet imbedded in the floor of the pickup. Now, these folks here have what looks like a .45 shot at their vehicle. They claim it was fired from your van. They have a bullet we can get tested. And, lo and behold, here we find you holding a .45."

"What are you saying?" Slim spat out.

"You're under arrest, Slim," Drake said. "For suspicion of murder of Dan White River. And you and Rob are both under arrest for the attempted murder of Cathy White River and Frank and Joe Hardy."

Chapter

13

"THIS IS NUTS!" Slim yelled. "I didn't shoot anybody! Someone else has been doing those shootings!"

"I guess it's just coincidence that you happen to be around when they take place," Joe said.

"That's right!" Slim said. "Is there a law against that?"

"You can practice your defense later, Slim," Burns said. He slipped a pair of handcuffs on Slim and another pair on Rob. Burns led the two off to the patrol car and pushed them into the backseat. Then he got into the front.

Drake turned to Cathy and the Hardys. "Well, I think we've got enough here to indict Slim. I'm glad you found that bullet," he said. "In the meantime, don't go too far from the area. The sheriff will want to talk to all of you." He nodded at them and walked to the patrol car.

"Sergeant Drake," Joe called out. Drake glanced back. "I was just wondering—did we get lucky here? Did you just happen to be passing through?"

Drake smiled. "Actually, you did get sort of lucky. Our radar picked up a couple of speeding vehicles. We were coming to give you a ticket. Guess we'll just let that go." Drake nodded toward the green van. "We'll send someone to get that later," he said. "You all drive safely now." He climbed into the patrol car, started the engine, and pulled out onto the road and disappeared.

Frank, Joe, and Cathy stood in the dusty road watching the patrol car go. "Well, maybe your father will get some justice now," Joe said quietly. Cathy seemed a little dazed by the turn of events. Finally she nodded and walked to the Hardys' van. Frank and Joe followed her.

Inside the van, Cathy said, "I'm sorry, guys. I just feel a little funny. I'm glad my father's killer has been caught, but I can't believe it was Slim. And I feel a little ashamed now about thinking Harry might have harmed my father. But it seemed so obvious in view of everything."

"There's no reason to be ashamed," Frank

said. "You had your reasons for suspecting him."

"I guess I was wrong about those," Cathy mused. "But I still feel there's more to this land business than we're being told. I just know John Pressel's got some kind of plan."

"Have you actually checked out the land in question?" Frank asked.

"I've been away at college most of this year," Cathy said. "I haven't seen it up close since Pressel began clearing it for Deadwood Days."

"Why don't we go take a peek now?" Frank suggested. "You can use our car phone to tell Harry about Slim's arrest. He can call Pressel and tell him the deal's back on. That'll stop the clock from running on the hundred-thousand-dollar-an-hour penalty."

Cathy nodded slowly. "I guess I'll have to. Frank started up the engine and after a little while Cathy said, "Take the next right up here, and we'll get a good view."

Frank turned right. They began to climb high in the Black Hills Forest. Soon larger, more angular rock formations took the place of rolling hills.

"Where are we going?" Joe asked.

Cathy smiled. "You'll see."

Cathy used the van's phone to call Harry at the reservation. Frank heard her explain the events of the past couple of hours. Then, after she listened for a minute or so, she said, "The decision is back in your hands, Harry. I just ask that you think about what I've said." She hung up, and the three drove along in silence for a while.

Then Joe sat up. "Wow!" he exclaimed. "Look at this!"

They had come to the very top of the mountain, where the trees had given way to a barren, rock-lined roadway. They could go no farther. Frank parked the van, and they all got out. They were standing on a small cliff—the highest point in the entire area. It looked out over the plateau, which appeared to be at least eight thousand feet below. Directly across, about five miles away, carved in the mountain, was a familiar sight.

"That's Mount Rushmore!" Joe yelled, pointing. The familiar faces of U.S. presidents Washington, Jefferson, Lincoln, and Theodore Roosevelt gleamed in the late afternoon sunshine. It was a breathtaking view. But there was more. Cathy turned and pointed above them. Frank and Joe raised their heads to see the unfinished Crazy Horse Memorial. An image of the great Sioux warrior atop his steed was being carved out of the face of an adjoining mountain.

"Crazy Horse is a little like the Native American Mount Rushmore," Cathy said. "It's not finished yet. But when it is, it'll be the tallest such sculpture in the United States—taller even than Rushmore."

Frank then stared down and out at the vista below. The plateau went on for miles. From there it appeared endless. Joe had retrieved a pair of binoculars from the van and was scanning the view.

Suddenly there was a loud explosion. "More dynamiting," Cathy said. She turned to Joe. "Could I use those for a moment?" she asked, indicating the binoculars. She peered through them at the plateau below.

"That's strange," Cathy said. "They're dynamiting in an area with no boulder formations."

"What does that mean?" Joe asked.

"There are only two reasons you use dynamite on the plateau," Cathy said. "One is to clear huge boulders or rocks. But there are none in that region."

"What's the other reason?" Frank asked.

"To uncover mineral deposits," Cathy said. "But if Pressel hasn't tested any ore yet, it doesn't make sense for him to keep blasting four or five times a day. That much dynamite is expensive."

"But why else would he be dynamiting?" Frank wondered.

"Why don't we go find out?" Joe said. They climbed back into the van, and Frank headed for the plateau. In fifteen minutes they had driven out of the Black Hills Forest and onto the desertlike flatland near the Black Cloud Reservation entrance.

"Go past here," Cathy said. "There's a turn-off about a half mile up. It takes you out to the area where they're doing the dynamiting."

"It still doesn't make sense to me," Joe said. "The secretary at the assayer's office was sure Pressel wasn't prospecting for gold. So how could his dynamiting be for anything other than clearing ground?"

"I just know what I saw," Cathy said. "And what I saw doesn't look like clearing ground. Whatever they're looking for, my bet is they haven't found it yet. I'd like to know what it is. And I'd like us to find it first."

They drove along the flat, dirt road, venturing farther and farther onto the wide, seemingly endless plateau. The ground shook again as a louder dynamite blast exploded. "We're getting closer," Joe said.

"Right now we're on the land that Pressel wants to keep so badly," Cathy said. "This is where my father planned to build our nature park."

Joe looked around. The land that stretched before them seemed untouched by time. At the line where the sharp blue sky met a light-colored plateau in the distance, Joe spotted a small herd of buffalo, dark dots moving in random patterns.

A moment later they came to a tall steel

fence. "What's this?" Frank asked. A sign on the fence read Deadwood Days Construction Site. No Admittance Without Proper Identification.

Behind the fence Frank saw various pieces of machinery whose function he could only guess at. A few workers were walking around, but they were too far away for Frank to see exactly what they were doing. Frank parked the van behind a hilly incline so it would be hidden from the entrance. The three of them jumped out.

Joe looked around. "Boy, this is like being on the moon." The landscape was flat, and the light-colored ground was hard and dusty, with a few patches of grass poking out. It was even more desolate than it was back on the Black Cloud Reservation, Joe thought.

"The mines around here appeared desolate, too, at one time," Cathy said. "Until someone discovered gold in them, and suddenly they weren't so desolate."

There was no one near the entrance area. The gate was locked and bolted. They could easily see inside, but getting in would be more difficult.

"Let's follow the fence as it curves around there," Joe said, pointing. "Maybe we can get a little closer to where they're dynamiting."

They walked around the corner of the fenced-off area. The machinery and workers were still about a half mile away, inside the construction site. Finally they stopped, and Cathy shook her head. "Take it from me as a mineralogy student. There's nothing out here but dirt and sand. The only reason Pressel has for dynamiting is to look for something."

Joe heard the crunch of car tires on the dirt and automatically hit the ground and rolled into the roadside ditch with Cathy and Frank. Rumbling along the dirt road toward the construction site was a dark-colored Cadillac. It left a trail of dust as it roared up to a gate in the fence about five hundred yards from where the Hardys and Cathy lay. The car stopped, and the gate automatically opened.

"I guess that driver has a remote for the gate," Frank said. The Cadillac entered, and the gate closed behind it. The car came to a stop and the front door opened. John Pressel stepped out. Standing with his back to the Hardys and Cathy, he glanced at his watch, then removed a hanky and mopped his brow in the late afternoon heat.

"I wonder what he's doing here?" Frank asked from their hiding place.

"It looks to me like he's waiting for someone," Joe said. A moment later another car could be heard rumbling along the dirt road. A truck drove up to the front gate. Across its side the name Leonard Gas, Inc., was printed in large letters.

The truck entered through the gate. As soon as it did, Pressel closed and rebolted it. "Leonard Gas?" Cathy said, squinting at the truck. "What is a gas company doing— Oh, wait a minute!" She gasped out loud.

"What is it?" Frank asked.

"Why didn't I think of this before!" Cathy exclaimed, her eyes wide with astonishment and her mouth hanging open.

Cathy slowly turned to the Hardys. "I should have guessed it from the very first. They're not looking for gold or silver or any kind of mineral. They think there's natural gas under this land!"

Chapter

14

"NATURAL GAS?" Joe said. "Would that be a big deal?"

"Big deal!" Cathy said, almost laughing. "Natural gas reserves are the most valuable find you can have today. Many industries are replacing other fuels with natural gas these days. If there's gas on this land, it could be worth billions! Certainly a whole lot more than what John Pressel's offering the tribe."

Joe turned back to watch Pressel talking with the two men who'd gotten out of the Leonard Gas truck. They started carrying equipment toward the other end of the plateau area. Cathy grabbed Joe's binoculars and stared through them.

"They're looking for gas reserves, all right,"

she declared. "It's a simple procedure. You blow a hole in the land, stick the gas meter down, and if your dial begins to move on the meter, you've found gas. They've probably already made some discoveries, and now they're searching for more. And natural gas isn't a mineral," she added excitedly. "It wouldn't be covered by the treaty. That's why Pressel was so desperate to close the deal before the land reverted to us."

"We're going to have to get some solid evidence," Frank pointed out. "If we can get you past that fence, can you perform the tests to confirm what you're saying?"

"Absolutely," Cathy said. "I can get a gauge. I did this test at school."

"But how do we get in here?" Joe asked. "Maybe we can come back at night—"

"I have a better idea," Cathy said. "Tomorrow they're going to reenact the Battle of Little Bighorn in the mesas near here. Everyone will be out there then. I can run the test, and no one will know the difference."

"Sounds good to me," Frank said.

"Do you guys ride horses?" she asked doubtfully.

"Do you have saddles?" Joe shot back.

Cathy smiled. "That depends. Are you going to ride with Custer or the Sioux?"

"I think we're on your side," Frank replied.

"I think you are, too," Cathy said. "For now,

can you get me back to the reservation? With Pressel here, I have a chance to talk to Harry alone. I have to tell him not to sign anything until we've had a chance to check this out."

"Let's go," Frank said. They hurried back to the van, and Joe turned it back onto the dirt road, not caring if Pressel saw them.

"It never occurred to me that Pressel could be searching for natural gas," Cathy said as the van bumped along. "Most of South Dakota's natural gas reserves have been found in the eastern part of the state."

"It's probably a good thing no one suspected there was gas here," Joe pointed out dryly. "If they had, there might have been treaties drawn up to make sure the tribes didn't get it, too."

They drove along in silence until Joe turned to Frank. "Is something on your mind?"

Frank came out of his reverie and nodded. "Yes, actually. Do either of you feel that Slim's arrest happened just a little too conveniently?"

"What do you mean?" Joe asked. "We saw him shooting at us. He was caught with the gun. And then there were the lab tests."

"We were *told* the lab tests were done," Frank said. "But you and I saw that truck, Joe. And Slim had plenty of time to go over it for evidence, inch by inch. How did the sheriff's people manage to find bullet fragments that all of us missed—and then get the test results so quickly? Those tests usually take longer."

"Do you think Drake and Burns were lying?" Cathy asked in surprise.

Frank shook his head. "I don't know. I just think they accepted our story pretty quickly. I mean, we didn't actually see who shot at us from the van. And Slim says he saw someone take his van. But Drake and Burns just overlooked those things and slapped handcuffs on Slim."

"Yeah, but you've seen how hot-tempered Slim is," Joe said. "And he was on the scene at both shootings."

"I know," Frank said. "But if Cathy is right about the natural gas, then there's a lot more at stake here than some ripped-up stock certificates. Think about it—a smart businessman like John Pressel could easily set up a hothead like Slim. You saw the way he handled him in the bank."

"Are you saying John Pressel had something to do with killing my father?" Cathy asked.

"I can't say anything for certain," Frank said. "But I think if we can get onto that restricted area tomorrow, we may solve more than one mystery around here."

Harry Leeds wasn't happy to see that Cathy had brought the Hardys onto the reservation again. But after inviting him to her house, she quickly explained what she had seen at the construction site.

"Harry, if Cathy's right about Pressel concealing natural gas reserves under that land, then you know you can't sign that land away. It would be like accepting pennies in exchange for a fortune," Frank pointed out.

"Every hour that goes by that I don't sign is costing our people one hundred thousand dollars," Harry said. "You're asking me to jeopardize that deal because Cathy thinks there's a possibility that there's natural gas under the land."

"Harry, I'm sure of it," Cathy said firmly.

Harry looked at Cathy, his dark, handsome features set in an expression of concentration. "All right, Cathy. I know you have the tribe's best interests at heart. And your college studies have taught you more about natural gas than I'll ever know," he said slowly. "I won't sign any deals with Pressel until you're satisfied we're not being cheated."

Cathy smiled at Harry. "That's the Harry Leeds I remember."

Harry turned to the Hardys. "You're welcome to spend the night as our guests on the reservation."

"Thank you. We'd be honored," Frank said.

"They're going to do more than that, Harry," Cathy said. "Tomorrow, at the battle of the Little Bighorn, they ride with the Sioux!"

After a well-earned dinner at Cathy's house, Frank and Joe spoke at length with Harry about their plan for the next day, then went to bed in one of the unoccupied cabins. Both were grateful to be able to sleep in a real bed after so many nights in sleeping bags. They rose early and had breakfast with Cathy and Sam White River.

"And now for the grand transformation to Sioux warriors," Cathy said, taking her dishes to the sink.

"I'm up for it," Joe said with a grin. "Just tell me what to do and wear."

"I've already thought of that." Smiling, Cathy motioned to the Hardys to follow her to her father's bedroom. Spread out on the bed were the traditional breeches, headbands, and leather vests that the Hardys had seen the Sioux tribe members wearing in the parade in Deadwood. There were also a couple of wooden hatchets—props for the battle, Joe supposed, as well as bows and quivers, with arrows sticking out of them.

"Uncle Sam managed to dig these up," Cathy told them mischievously. "Put the clothes on while I change in the bathroom. Then, if I feel like it, maybe I'll try putting a little war paint on you, too."

A few minutes later Frank and Joe were back in the living room, admiring themselves in their unfamiliar clothes. "Very cool," Joe said, sliding his hatchet into his leather waistband. He also slid a metal cutting tool that

Cathy had given him into the waistband. Not authentic, he thought, but he'd need it later.

"Doesn't look so cool to me," Sam White River teased, sipping from a cup of coffee. "You boys look pale to me."

"We'll get plenty of sun today, Uncle." Cathy entered the room in her own traditional clothing—the same clothes she'd worn in the parade. She handed the boys their bows and quivers, then slung her own over her shoulder. "Wish us luck in defeating Mr. Custer—and hope we'll be back with good news for you tonight."

Cathy gave her uncle a kiss and led the two Hardys out to the van. "Now for your mighty steeds," she said.

"What about war paint?" Joe protested.

"No time." Cathy tossed a lipstick over her shoulder to him. "But you're welcome to do what you can with that."

More than two dozen men, women, and children, many in traditional clothing, were tending the horses and chatting when Cathy and the Hardys arrived at the corral. Cathy picked out two horses for Frank and Joe and then brought out her own brown-and-white Appaloosa. She and the Hardys mounted their horses and rode toward the entrance to the reservation.

Over a hundred Black Cloud tribe members had gathered near the reservation entrance, most riding horses bareback, but several dozen more were packed into cars and trucks. The Sioux were all dressed in the type of clothing their ancestors had worn on that famous day in 1876 when they had defeated Custer. They had two painted stripes under each eye. To Joe, the bravest looking of all was Harry Leeds. He would play the role of Crazy Horse, the legendary Sioux warrior who had led his people to their victory.

The group filed out of the reservation entrance and headed toward the plains area. Frank's heart began to beat a little faster. Though he knew it was only a reenactment, the sight of the proud Sioux atop their horses, armed, painted, and riding across an open plain, brought chills.

In a short time the tribe members had gathered at the bottom of the canyon where the battle was to be reenacted. A narrow river ran along the canyon floor, and dozens of authentic tepees had been erected along its winding banks. A large group of tourists were crowded inside a spectator section on one slope of the mesa lining the canyon. Custer's forces had assembled to the east on the opposite side, at the lip of the facing plateau. They were dressed in replicas of the U.S. cavalry uniforms worn by the soldiers of 1876. Frank spotted Murph from the diner, Mr. Carter from Town Hall, and even Slim's friend Doug among the cavalry group. A compact man on horseback near the front, disguised in a long blond wig and mustache, was clearly playing George Armstrong Custer.

"In the real battle, Custer started out with about six hundred soldiers," Cathy explained to the Hardys as they dismounted with the tribe members and dispersed among the tepees. "They came riding along the top of the mesa and spotted a Hunkpapa Sioux village down below. Planning to ambush it, Custer split his forces into three sections. He figured there could be as many as fifteen hundred warriors in the village. What he didn't realize was that around a bend in the mesa, past where he could see, were five thousand more Sioux from half a dozen different tribes, and at least two thousand warriors ready to fight."

"Did the women fight, too?" Joe asked, looking skeptically at Cathy's warriorlike breeches and vest.

"Of course not. Their job was to protect the children." Cathy grinned and tossed her head. "But this is my fifth Little Bighorn reenactment, Joe. If there's one thing I've learned, it's that the role of warrior is more fun."

A microphone had been set up near the spectators' area. John Pressel, the emcee, slowly approached the mike.

"My friends, today we will be reenacting a well-known moment in our nation's history—the Battle of Little Bighorn," Pressel announced, his voice ringing up and down the canyon. "This will be the final event of this special Wild West Week. I hope you have enjoyed the festivities. Of course, our week has been marred by the terrible loss of a friend and a leader in the Black Hills community. Dan White River of the Black Cloud tribe was killed in a tragic auto accident. He will be missed by all who knew him. I'd like to dedicate this final event to his memory."

Pressel put down the microphone and returned to his troops. Cathy turned to Frank, shook her head, and muttered "hypocrite" under her breath.

Over the loudspeaker came the sound of a lively frontier song from the late 1800s. In the canyon below, Cathy smiled at the Hardys and motioned to them to help her add wood to a campfire. Other tribe members were pretending to wash clothes in the river, tend to children, confer in front of tepees, and otherwise act out the roles of unsuspecting Sioux. Joe exchanged a grin with Harry Leeds, who was calmly whittling a piece of wood. It was clear the tribe members were enjoying the game.

Suddenly, from above, a trumpet sounded, and the battle was on.

Joe heard the first division of cavalrymen yell as they charged down toward the village. Reacting instantly, he raced toward his horse along with his brother and Cathy. Sioux women and children screamed, running away, as Pressel's amplified voice described for the spectators what was happening. The cavalry unit arrived at the floor of the canyon. Harry Leeds rose up on his horse, gave a bloodcurdling cry, and led the counterattack.

With the first clash of forces more than two dozen soldiers fell to the ground, while only two tribe members were "wounded." Joe's pulse raced as he brandished his wooden hatchet and hung on to his horse's mane, pretending to sink his weapon into one cavalryman after another. He had decided to forget about pretending to use the bow and arrows. After the first rush the two forces separated, the cavalry retreating as the Sioux rode deeper into the canyon to warn their brothers and, unknowingly, meet Custer himself.

Frank, Joe, and Cathy survived the first assault. "Okay, this is the one we break on," Frank said quietly as the trio rode breathlessly around the slight bend in the canyon. More tepees were set up here, and more "warriors" were just now rushing to their horses.

"When Custer leads the charge down the side of the mesa, we ride right through the army line to the top," Frank continued. "That plateau marks the border of Pressel's land. We should be able to make it to the construction site in under ten minutes by horseback. Are we ready?" Joe and Cathy nodded. In the distance a cavalry trumpet sounded the second charge again, and Harry Leeds responded with a terrifying yell.

As the Sioux warriors galloped up the slope of the mesa, picking off Custer's men under trees and in arroyos, no one seemed to notice the three combatants riding through the cavalry's line and galloping uphill. Once they reached the top of the plateau, Frank, Joe, and Cathy tore off, speeding straight toward the Deadwood Days construction site.

When they reached the fence, they looked around cautiously. "Looks like no one's here," Frank said, peering in. The machinery was still in the same place it had been yesterday.

"Let's get to work," Joe said. He slid off his horse, dropped his hatchet, and took out the pair of metal-cutting shears. It was harder than Joe had anticipated to clip the lock on the front gate, but finally, the gate swung open. Joe jumped back on his horse, and the three of them rode into the restricted area.

"I want to go to where the dynamiting is being done," Cathy said. "That way I'll know for sure what's going on here."

The area resembled a bomb site, Joe thought. Whole sections had been blown up, and gaping holes punctuated the earth. "This doesn't look like a construction area to me," he said.

Cathy got off her horse and took a long metal rod from her quiver. At the top of the rod was a circular meter. Frank and Joe dismounted, too, and joined Cathy where she knelt on the ground. She was pushing the pipelike projection into the ground. Once it was in two feet deep, she stopped.

"This will detect any gas formations underground," Cathy said. "If there's even a trace of natural gas within a hundred feet of this meter, this instrument will pick it up."

"How long does it take to do that?" Frank asked.

Cathy looked up to respond and caught her breath. Frank jerked his head around to see Forest Patrol sergeants Drake and Burns sneaking up on them from behind a pile of debris. They weren't wearing their uniforms.

"Well, kids, we'd really hoped it wouldn't come to this," Drake said. Burns nodded, a smarmy smile on his face. "But some people just can't help getting themselves in trouble."

"What's going on?" Joe demanded.

Drake jerked his .38 out of his waistband. "What's going on is that your little 'investigation' just went one step too far," he growled. "And now you're going to have to pay for it."

Chapter

15

FRANK, JOE, AND CATHY froze in place. Frank stared at the gun in Drake's hand, glinting in the sunlight.

Suddenly Cathy's voice broke the tense silence. "Look, I know we're trespassing," she said, "but we had—"

"They're not here because we're trespassing," Frank said. Cathy turned sharply to him.

"What?" she said.

Frank looked at Drake as he spoke. "They're here to protect their real boss—John Pressel."

Drake didn't move a muscle as he stared back at Frank. "Clever to the end, aren't you?"

"Not too clever," Burns put in. "Or he wouldn't be standing there looking so dopey." He laughed, gesturing with his own gun at the Hardys' and Cathy's clothes.

"Maybe you're not familiar with Mr. Pressel's trespassing policy," Drake said. "Shoot first, ask questions later. Now, I'm going to count to three. My advice would be for you kids to make a run for it. I hear it's less painful to be shot in the back. One—two—"

Frank saw Cathy's brown and white horse standing behind Drake and Burns. Suddenly he had an idea. As quickly as he could, he made the thumbs-up sign that Cathy had used in the rodeo competition. The Appaloosa tensed when he saw the signal.

"Thr—" Drake began.

Frank rolled his hands one over the other, and the horse came charging at Drake and Burns from the rear. Frank grabbed Joe and Cathy and pulled them to the ground.

"Hey!" Drake shouted. As he hit the dusty ground, Frank heard the sound of gunfire.

"What are you—!" Cathy protested, struggling to stand up again.

Frank looked up in time to see Cathy's horse charge toward them between Drake and Burns, knocking the two men to the ground. Their guns went flying from their hands.

In a flash Joe had jumped a dazed Burns. Burns swung wildly with his right hand and missed. Joe came up underneath and caught the officer with a left hook to the ribs. The blow sent Burns reeling.

Frank ran over to Drake. The smaller man was quicker than his partner, and he scrambled for his gun, which was lying a few feet away. He grabbed it and held it on Frank. "Okay, freeze where you are!" Drake yelled at Frank. "You, too!" he yelled over to Joe. "Now! Or your brother gets it right between the eyes!"

Joe had no choice. He let Burns go. Breathing heavily, Burns staggered over to Drake. Cathy, who had jumped up to retrieve her horse, now stood still, trying to calm the jittery animal.

"Two high school kids," Drake muttered, brushing himself off. He glared at Frank and Joe in contempt. "Did you really think you were going to stop John Pressel?"

"They've been on Pressel's payroll the whole time," Joe said to himself.

"Nothing gets by you, does it, Slick?" Drake said. He moved a step closer, leveling the gun directly at Joe's head.

"That's why they were so concerned about someone panning for gold near our camping site," Frank said. "If any gold was found in that stream, it would have been washed down from the Hills into the plateau. They were looking out for Pressel's interests."

"Then they were the ones who killed my father," Cathy said, her voice a mixture of amazement and anger.

"That's how they managed to be on the scene so quickly," Frank said, speaking more quickly now. "They set it up to frame Slim Davenport. They must have called, requesting a battery to be sent to Spearfish. That way Slim would be in the Hills when Dan White Feather was driving through. They made sure to use a .45 bullet on the truck's front tire. Without White River, Pressel could pull off his land sale with the Black Cloud tribe. And Slim Davenport would be in jail, arrested for the crimes they'd committed."

"That's enough," Drake said, turning to Frank. "None of that matters now."

Frank ignored him, too caught up in solving the mystery to listen. "When we started getting in their way, they decided to beef up their case against Slim and get rid of us at the same time," he said to Joe and Cathy. "They followed us, shot at our tires, and framed Slim for it."

"So Slim wasn't lying. His van really had been stolen," Joe said.

"And these are the thieves," Frank said. "You guys must have had your patrol car parked near the reservation, knowing that we'd have to take Cathy home that way. When we met up with Slim, you were close by, ready to arrest him."

"But how did they get Slim's van?" Cathy asked.

"Older vans aren't hard to hot-wire, are they, Drake?" Frank said. He stared at the officer. "Have I made any mistakes yet?"

"Just one," Drake said. "You figured no one would follow you out here today. But like I said, we're here to make sure nothing keeps Mr. Pressel's deal from going through. That's what he pays us for."

Suddenly Frank pulled a small tape recorder from his pocket. "Thanks for letting us get all this on tape," Frank said. "You know what they say. A good detective never leaves home without one."

For a moment Drake's face froze. Then slowly he laughed, and Burns followed suit.

"Too bad you're never going to get to play it for anybody," Burns said.

"I wouldn't be sure about that," Frank said, a smile crossing his face.

Frank, Joe, and Cathy all pointed behind Drake and Burns. A low rumbling in the distance was growing louder and louder.

From across the plateau, the Black Cloud tribe came racing. They pushed toward Pressel's gate on horseback, a huge cloud of dust billowing up behind them. Harry Leeds led the way, leaning low over the neck of his horse.

"Time to give it up, Drake," Frank said quietly. He watched a trickle of sweat slide down Drake's pale face. The officer looked back at the Sioux, now a loud, dusty mass rushing toward them. Drake lowered his gun and dropped it. Burns did the same.

Moments later Harry Leeds galloped up to the group and reined his horse to a halt.

"What took you so long?" Frank asked as more of the Sioux warriors joined them. "I was starting to get a little worried."

"Sorry," Harry said breathlessly, wiping dust from his forehead with his arm. "We got held up by the cavalry. Everything work out okay?"

Frank held up the tape recorder. "We got our evidence and confession." He nodded toward Drake and Burns. "And I think they've got a few things they need to tell the authorities."

Several of the Black Cloud tribe members dismounted, grabbed Drake and Burns, and led them to the Forest Patrol car near the gate to use the officers' radio.

Harry Leeds slid off his horse. "How could you have been so sure they'd try to stop you out here?" Harry asked.

"Joe and I weren't sure at all," Frank said with a grin. "But I figured if Cathy was right and there was a reserve of natural gas under this land, then either she'd find it or somebody would be on the property and try to stop her from finding it, in which case we might need additional help. As it turned out, we got it both ways." Frank turned to Cathy. "You got a positive reading, right?"

Cathy checked the gauge, smiled brightly, and nodded. Then she turned to Frank and Joe. "How can I ever thank you for your help?"

"You can thank this fellow more than us," Frank said, nodding at Cathy's horse. "He saved all of us. And of course, we all put on a pretty good act for Drake and Burns."

"You're being modest," Harry Leeds said. "The entire Black Cloud tribe owes you a debt of gratitude. I was prepared to sign a deal with Pressel that would have cost us millions of dollars. Now we're going to keep this land."

He turned to Cathy and spoke simply but with great emotion. "And I promise the first thing we'll do with the income from the natural gas reserves is construct a nature park on a section of the land. I even have a name for it: the Dan White River Nature Preserve."

Cathy's eyes shone as she blinked back her tears.

"Hey, what about Pressel?" Joe suddenly said. "Someone's got to make sure he doesn't get away—"

"He won't," Harry said from atop his horse. "When he saw us riding out here, he knew something was wrong. I spotted him from the top of the plateau, running for his car."

"What happened then?" Frank asked.

"He didn't get very far," Harry said. "He was tackled by one of his own cavalry, who apparently was keeping an eye on him. Pressel's on his way to the Deadwood sheriff's office right now."

"Who tackled him?" Joe asked, fascinated.

"I don't think you know him," Harry said. "His name's Murph. He runs a restaurant in town." Harry nodded to the Hardys, then he and the other Sioux rode off, heading back toward the spectator grounds.

"I hope your father can rest in peace now," Frank said to Cathy.

"I think he will," Cathy said with a sad smile. "Now that his dream will come true."

Joe jumped back on his horse. "Well, they may have taken Pressel away, but we've still got a battle to win back there."

Cathy smiled. "You're right. Race you back!"

But before they left, Joe turned to Frank. "I just realized something," he said.

"What?" Frank asked impatiently.

"Nothing much. Just that if we left right now, we might be able to get you back to Bayport before Callie notices you're late," Joe said.

Frank laughed. "How often do you get to *win* the Battle of the Little Big Horn? Callie will have to understand if we're a few hours late getting home."

Frank jumped on his horse, and he and Joe rode off, the wide plateau ahead of them.

Frank and Joe's next case:

The Hardys have come to Alaska's Denali National Park to experience the awesome power of America's final wilderness. But in the face of a disastrous series of forest fires, they discover that the true test of survival will pit them not against natural forces—but against human evil. For the fires have been deliberately set!

With crime—and the flames—raging out of control, the boys leap into action, joining a crack team of parachuting firefighters. They uncover a trail of destruction, greed, and arson for profit, which leads them directly into the line of fire. The sparks are flying, and Frank and Joe are about to descend into the fight of their lives ... in *Inferno of Fear,* Case #88 in the Hardy Boys Casefiles™.

For orders other than by individual consumers, Archway Books grants a discount on the purchase of **10 or more** copies of single titles for special markets or premium use. For further details, please write to the Vice-President of Special Markets, Pocket Books, 1230 Avenue of the Americas, New York, NY 10020.

For information on how individual consumers can place orders, please write to Mail Order Department, Paramount Publishing, 200 Old Tappan Road, Old Tappan, NJ 07675.